THE LEAGUE OF
UNITED
PLANETS

THE LEAGUE OF UNITED PLANETS

LONNIE C. LARSON

The League of United Planets

Copyright © 2022 by Lonnie C. Larson. All rights reserved.

No part of this publication may be reproduced, stored in a retrieval system or transmitted in any way by any means, electronic, mechanical, photocopy, recording or otherwise without the prior permission of the author except as provided by USA copyright law.

The opinions expressed by the author are not necessarily those of URLink Print and Media.

1603 Capitol Ave., Suite 310 Cheyenne, Wyoming USA 82001
1-888-980-6523 | admin@urlinkpublishing.com

URLink Print and Media is committed to excellence in the publishing industry.

Book design copyright © 2022 by URLink Print and Media. All rights reserved.

Published in the United States of America

Library of Congress Control Number: 2022914667
ISBN 978-1-68486-245-0 (Paperback)
ISBN 978-1-68486-246-7 (Digital)

02.08.22

Dedicated to Steffanie and Jonny Larson.

CHAPTER ONE

A few days after Gheron's son-in-law Bob left for Pogh to start his search for Leah, he sat down in his study and started working on a plan that he hoped, would bring together the civilized planets in this sector. The first thing that he did was to collect and study as much information about the "United Nations" on Earth that he could find in the archives. After much study, he carefully selected bits and parts and then set about creating a simple set of guidelines that could easily be accepted and adopted by the many civilized races in this sector. Gheron spent several months, painstakingly piecing together this document and then he set about contacting the nearby systems.

Gheron's first stop, naturally, was to go see President Tom Morrow of Pogh and present him with his son-in- law's idea.

"Welcome Gheron, please sit," President Morrow said.
"Thank you for seeing me Mr. president," Gheron said.
"What I am about to propose might sound a bit ridiculous or fanciful; but I believe, in time, this idea can/will become the cornerstone for a great alliance between all of the civilized systems in this sector and quite possibly the whole quadrant."

"Sounds interesting. Tell me all about it," President Morrow said.

"My proposal is this; we contact the systems close to Pogh and ask them if they would be willing to join a Unification of Planets, so to speak, where all of the member systems pledge to help and defend each other in times of battle or natural disasters. After the destruction of home world, Berillion, about nine years ago; it had been brought to my attention that if there had been an alliance of worlds in place back then, perhaps Berillion would not have been destroyed so easily. Since then I have spent many a month thinking about that remark. And what I have come up with is a set of simple guidelines that should be compatible with, and complimentary to, most of the known system's preexisting laws."

"As you are well aware, before Berillion was destroyed by the Cyborgs, our two worlds enjoyed a peaceful trade agreement. We were able to benefit from each others strengths and enhance each others weaknesses. Our knowledge of science, medicine and the arts along with your knowledge of defenses and manufacturing combined to form quite a nice little pact of our own. The only thing missing between our systems was an agreement to come to each others aid, should there have been a natural disaster or, in our case, an attack by an outside alien force."

"Using the premise of that loose alliance that we shared, and what my son-in-law told me about the nations of his home world sharing a similar alliance, I propose to try and duplicate that with as many civilized systems in this sector that I can. Adding in the agreement to come to the aid of each other. Now, I know it won't be easy but nothing worthwhile ever is. So, Mr. President, what do you think?"

"I believe that what you propose could be very beneficial. But you do understand, Gheron, that the World Council of Pogh will have to discuss this matter in great length before we can agree to join into any such agreement," Morrow stated.

"I understand completely Mr. President," Gheron said. "All I am asking is that you take your time and review it; and while the World Council takes this matter under consideration, I will use that time to go to Deron to speak to President Day."

"I know it may be difficult, but you have all of the information you need before you and if you have any concerns, you can contact me anytime and I trust that you will do your best. I truly hope that when I return we will have the start of something greater than any of us could possibly imagine."

"I understand the importance of this matter and I couldn't agree more. I assure you, I will do my best to try to convince the council of that. I wish you the best of luck on this journey Gheron," president Morrow said as he shook Gheron's hand and then walked him to the door.

"Thank you Mr. President," Gheron said as he walked out of their meeting.

Gheron wasted little time preparing for the trip to Deron and soon he was off. When he arrived and finally met with president Day, he was told virtually the same thing; that a decision couldn't be made without the full support of their world leaders as well.

Gheron had spent the better part of two years traveling between Pogh and Deron; giving testimony and answering questions and explaining, as best he could, why this would be a good thing for everyone involved. Finally Gheron was informed that both Pogh and Deron would agree to sign the charter. Gheron asked each of their leaders to choose an ambassador that could represent them at the High Council and help him in his quest to sign up other worlds in other systems.

And so with that done, Gheron, along with Joshua and Cheran, the ambassadors from Pogh and Deron respectively, left for the planet Thoria in the Borjoue system to speak to the High Leader, Tahl.

As soon as Gheron's ship was within communication range he contacted the government and told them that they were on a diplomatic mission and respectfully requested a meeting with Tahl, the High Leader of Thoria.

Within a week after arrival Gheron, Joshua and Cheran were meeting with Tahl.

All three of them took their turns explaining the basic idea of the charter and all of the benefits that it held to Thoria. Tahl had many questions for the three diplomats and they answered them as best they could "What is in it for Thoria?" Tahl finally asked.

"If I may," Joshua stated. "Pogh and Berillion have enjoyed a trade agreement with each other for nearly three centuries now. We have defense and manufacturing prowess whereas Berillion, up until its recent destruction, had medical, scientific and cultural arts knowledge that our two worlds shared equally. The only difference between then and the present, is that now our worlds have entered into a formal alliance to promise to defend each other and to provide aid during times of natural disaster…"

"Berillion does not exist anymore since the Cyborg attack," Tahl said. "What have they got to offer us now that they no longer have any of those things?" He asked.

"Pogh alone has over five hundred thousand refugees from Berillion that have successfully assimilated into our civilization," Joshua explained. "Even though there is no physical Berillion home world, there still is a great Berillion presence in this sector. Their people still have a great deal of knowledge to offer other worlds."

"What of Deron?" Tahl asked as he turned his attention to Cheran.

"Deron has a defense force that is capable of defeating an attack from almost any hostile race," Cheran said. "We too were attacked by the Cyborg creatures nearly a year after Berillion was destroyed and we successfully defeated them. However, it came at a very high cost to the people of Deron. Most of our assets were put into defense and we did not have enough resources left over for much of our needed infrastructure because of that."

"It is taking time and we are slowly rebuilding. And I am certain that this alliance between the planet Deron, the planet Pogh and the vast "knowledge" held by the Berillion refugees, on both our worlds, will help to speed up that recovery and further strengthen our planets entire infrastructure."

"We have virtually the same amount of knowledge and capabilities as the Berillions have," Tahl said. "Why do we need to ally ourselves with your three races?"

"Because of that very statement," Gheron said as he stood up. "If we, Berillion, were not able to defeat our enemy with all of the resources at our disposal, then it would seem likely that you could suffer the same fate should these alien Cyborg creatures decide to continue attacking and destroying the worlds of this sector."

"But if you were to join us, and become a member of the charter you would have access to a vastly stronger defense system as well as medical and scientific research. Your world would fall under its protection clause."

"I believe I understand now, thank you. You have all made strong and valid points," Tahl said. "I shall bring this up for deliberation by the World Council. You will be contacted if and when we reach a decision. Until that time you are welcome to stay here and enjoy what Thoria has to offer.

"Thank you your Excellence, your offer is generous and greatly appreciated but we feel that we need to continue contacting as many worlds as we can before we are faced with another enemy race bent on total destruction," Gheron said.

"I understand," Tahl said. "I will contact Pogh and Deron as soon as we have reached a decision. Goodbye and good luck to you all."

Gheron, Cheran and Joshua said goodbye to Tahl and then headed for the planet Orion in the Trifid nebula. The Thorian council studied and debated the proposal at great length…

CHAPTER TWO

The trip to Orion took eighteen months and as soon as Gheron's ship had docked the three delegates made their way to the High Ruler, Aaron's, office. Orion had just recently entered the faster than light age and if ever there was a world that could benefit from an alliance it would be this world and worlds just like this one. Orion was predominately an agricultural world with a moderately low population but despite this, they did have a lot to offer the League as well.

"How is it a young race such as ours can be of service to you and this League you speak of?" Aaron asked.

"You underestimate your potential," Gheron said. "It is because you are a young race with an agriculture base that interests me. Your world has entered into a new age, now that you have developed your faster then light engines.

You are now vulnerable; if your world signed on with the League it would fall under the protection of no less then three races worth of knowledge and experience at this time. Your citizens could/would learn much and all that would be asked for in return is your experience and knowledge in agriculture."

"How can I be sure that you are not a threat to our world now? And that you won't just attack and then take our resources?" Aaron asked.

"That is a valid concern, but you can be assured that no one here is going to be a threat to your people or attack your world," Joshua interjected. "We believe in this alliance and we believe it could benefit all the civilized worlds in this sector."

"All we are doing here, right now, is offering you the opportunity to study our world's histories, which we have included, and the guidelines that Gheron has drafted for this League charter. If your World Council decides not to join, you can be assured that we will not harm you and that we will leave you in peace. All we ask is that you study the charter so that you can make an educated decision."

"Thank you for that," Aaron said. "It may take some time for the Council to review all the information you have provided. Please take the opportunity to rest and explore what Orion has to offer. I will try my best to see if I can speed that process up."

"Thank you Aaron," Cheran said. "We can only stay for a short time before we need to move on, we have many more worlds to contact."

With that, Aaron excused himself and had his aid show them out. Gheron contacted Thoria and discovered that the High Council had agreed to sign the League charter and that a representative had been sent to Pogh as an ambassador.

"Now there are five," Gheron said.

"I thought Thoria was only the third outside world you contacted," Cheran said.

"Yes it is. But there is the first," Gheron said. "I have kept it secret and with all due respect I wish to keep it that way until I can be sure this League of United Planets is successful."

"Understood," Cheran said and with that he went out to find what the city had to offer.

"Understood here as well," Joshua said and he too went out for the evening.

While they were on Orion, Joshua met a woman, her name was Jade and she would take him on tours of the city and tell him all about Orion. Every day that they spent together they found themselves falling more and more in love. One day Joshua called upon Gheron to ask if it would be Okay to marry her.

Gheron was happy for him.

"I can not tell you what is right for you," Gheron said. "Only you and Jade can tell what is in your hearts. If you love each other as you say then there is room enough on our ship."

Joshua and Jade were married a month later and unbeknownst to anyone; one of their wedding gifts was from Aaron and it was a copy of the signed charter with Orion. A few days later Gheron met with Aaron and the Ambassador that was chosen to represent Orion, her name was Cassandra, he thanked Aaron and welcomed Cassandra and when she was ready, they departed and headed back to Pogh.

Gheron was very eager to have plans made up for a central meeting place where the delegates from the planets could officially conduct their business. He had visions for a League Council Chambers on each of the member planets as well. While he was on Pogh he dropped Joshua and Jade off and then picked up the new delegate, Lloyd from Thoria and when they were ready they took off for the planet Dobro in the Altaries system.

The trip to Dobro took about six months and Gheron used the ship as a makeshift Council chambers. While en- route, the guidelines of the charter were refined and re- tuned to enhance each of the member planets capabilities. By the time Gheron reached Dobro the League was working smoothly as could be expected for only being a few years old. As soon as they were within range Gheron contacted the Prime Minister of Dobro, Camille, and asked her for an audience.

Gheron, Cassandra, Lloyd and Cheran met with Camille and presented her with all of the information on the League charter to date, and then they explained what it would mean for the people of her world. Then they told her that they would stay on Dobro for as long as it was necessary to answer any questions and address any concerns that she or their Council might have for them.

It seemed that the most asked questions, so far, were; why join? And, what is in it for us?

After explaining all of the benefits that Dobro would have and answering all of their questions, Gheron, Cassandra, Lloyd and Cheran left the Council so that they might deliberate. The small band of delegates made their way to the quarters that were provided for them and waited. From time to time the High Council would have a few questions that needed to be answered in more detail so one or more of the delegates would go and answer them.

While they waited for the High Council's decision they took this time to put even more information into the charter proposal in hopes to speed up the decision making process and to try and make it less confusing for other worlds in the future.

Finally, after six months of deliberating, the High Council of Dobro agreed to sign on. Camille called the delegates into her office and introduced them to Candace, Dobro's new ambassador to the League, and when Candace was ready to leave, they all headed for Pogh.

Back on Pogh, the new Ambassadors were given six months to settle into their new quarters before they were sent out to recruit new members. Gheron took this time to have all of the information about the League charter placed on computer note pads and then it was time to get to work. After giving the new Ambassadors their copies he sent each of them on their way.

Gheron sent Joshua and his wife Jade to the planet Aldebaran in the Aquarius system, Candace and Cheran went to the planet Valor in the Hahn system, Lloyd and Cassandra went to the planet Osiris in the Paccard system and he alone went to the planet Vergon located in the Pegasus system.

CHAPTER
THREE

Gheron's trip to Vergon took eighteen months and he used the time to plan out in detail what he was going to say and how he was going to say it. The Vergon race was by far the oldest known race in this part of the galaxy; they rarely ventured out, so to say that he was nervous would be an understatement.

When Gheron's ship entered the system he received word from their Central Space Control that he was expected and then he was given the coordinates for landing. This made Gheron even more nervous.

When Gheron landed he was driven out to a small modest house just outside the city proper. This house was not at all like the houses he had just passed along the way. It was a very simple structure, almost small by comparison. The small lawn was neatly manicured and the pathway leading up to the front door was simply concrete. And when Gheron walked up and knocked on the door, it wasn't a servant that answered, it was a tall stout man, plainly, but neatly dressed.

"I have been expecting you Ambassador Gheron, welcome to Vergon," he stated as he opened the door.

Gheron was surprised and simply said, "You have me at a disadvantage sir."

"I apologize," the man said. "My name is William Mont, and I have been given the privilege of being the Vergon ambassador to the League of United Planets. Please have a seat."

Gheron was stunned. "How is this possible?" He asked as he sat down. "It has only just begun."

"We have been watching your progress for the past few years now," William said. "We knew it was only a matter of time before you would contact us."

"I wasn't even sure if I should," Gheron said. "I only just decided to come here at the last minute. No one on my staff even knew I was coming here."

"We knew," William said. "This League of United Planets of yours is past due in coming. It should have happened centuries ago. So tell me Gheron, when did you decide to start it?"

"Almost ten years ago now," Gheron answered. "After Berillion was destroyed and I had a lengthy conversation with my son-in-law."

"So, it is his idea then?" William asked. "Where is he? I should like to meet him."

"Sort of," Gheron said. "And he is not here. He is out searching for Leah, his wife and my daughter."

"You said "sort of. What do you mean by that?" William asked.

"Well. During one of our many visits, before he went to search for Leah, he had told me something and it struck a chord. I never would have thought that someone so young could be so wise."

"Young?" William asked. "You are an old race. Not nearly as old as ours but still very old. How can someone from your world be considered young?"

Before he had time to think Gheron simply answered, "My son-in-law is not a Berillion, he is a human from Earth."

"Robert!" was all William said, not as a question but more like a statement of fact.

If Gheron had not already been sitting down he would surely have fallen over. "Wwwhyy yeeess," Gheron stammered. "Hhow could you possibly know that?" "I had a feeling about Robert too, when I first met him," William said.

"What? You have met Bob? When? Where?" Gheron asked. "Has he been here recently?"

"First, yes I have met Bob, and second no, Bob has never been to Vergon," William said. "I met him on Earth many years before you did."

Now Gheron was starting to get frightened.

"Do not worry," William said. "We Vergons had known about your "accidental" landing on Earth and since I was already there, I had been given the task of protecting you and getting you back to Berillion safely. But before I could do that, Bob got to you first; and as he would say, the rest is history."

"But if you knew that we needed help then why didn't you step in and help?" Gheron asked.

"Well," William started. "Call it a gut feeling. You see I sensed something in Bob a long time ago and I wanted to, no, I had to see if it were true. Let me tell you a little something about your son-in-law that you probably did not know. I met him for the first time about five years before your ship crashed on Earth. The Vergon race has been monitoring Earth's progress for several thousands of years now and I was staying on Earth as a sheriff's deputy; the dispatch had received an emergency call late one night for a traffic accident out near Bob's farm. When I arrived on scene I saw Bob treating a man that had severe bleeding from a large cut on his leg."

"I knew Bob from around town. He was a straight up kind of man and many of the folks around town like him a lot. Every time that we would meet I could sense something that I cannot divulge at this time. Anyway, I identified myself as I approached and Bob quickly yelled at me to get the damned ambulance there as fast as possible. He told me that the man's femoral artery had been cut and that he would bleed to death in minutes."

"As I approached them I recognized the injured man as Chester, he owned a bar and restaurant in town, and I saw that Bob was holding his artery closed with his hand. The ambulance had to come from the next city and it would take them at least twenty minutes to get there. Bob knew this and he told me to contact the dispatcher and request a medical helicopter and to have them notify the hospital also."

"Bob said that the hospital needed to have an operating room and doctors standing by and ready to operate the second that they arrived. The helicopter was there in less than ten minutes. The flight surgeon wanted to take over but Bob just told him that he had come this far and he wasn't about to let go of Chester's artery until they were safely in the operating room and the doctors were sewing him up."

"When they got to the hospital they went directly to the operating room and one of the doctors told Bob that he had to leave now because he wasn't sterile. Bob just laughed and said that it was not going to make much difference now, as he had been holding Chester's artery with his gloved hand for at least a good half hour now. He told the doctor that Chester's wound was as dirty as it was gonna be. Then Bob told a nurse to just wrap a gown around him and around his arm and start working."

"Once prepped, the surgeon opened Chester's leg to expose more of the artery and started stitching it closed and after about two hours of operating, he was finished and then he told Bob to let off the pressure. Bob slowly released his grip and watched to see if the stitches held and when he saw that they did he released his grip completely and then he left the operating room to get cleaned up while the surgeon finished stitching up Chester's leg."

"I had driven over to the hospital, and I waited for an update on Chester's condition. When the doctor came out, he said that if it had not been for Bob's quick thinking and his actions, Chester would have died. When I finally found Bob he was staring out a window drinking a cup of coffee. I offered him a ride home and he accepted. On the drive back I asked him where he had learned his first aid training and he told me from the Marine Corps."

"We talked on the drive back and I got to know a little more about him. When we got back to his farm he turned to me and apologized for yelling at me earlier. I told him not to worry about it and then I told him that he had a damn good reason to. Then I said just don't do it again and he just said, "I'll do it as long as it takes." I looked over at Bob and then I laughed and so did he. We became good friends."

"About a month later the city had a special ceremony and Bob was presented with two certificate of outstanding merit one from the city and one from the sheriffs department. After that, Bob never had to pay for another drink or meal whenever he stopped in at Chester's; oh he tried to pay but Chester would kindly throw him out. Bob would figure out how much it cost and he would put that much in the tip jar on the bar anyway."

"Bob was always the first in line if someone needed help, it didn't matter when, where, what or why, he was always there. He never asked for anything in return. Then one night a fire destroyed one of Bob's buildings. He had spent the whole of the next day driving around collecting estimates from several lumberyards for replacement costs. When he stopped by his insurance agency with the quotes, his agent took the highest one and cut him a check right there. And when Bob returned home later that afternoon the burned out shed was completely gone and the things that were salvageable were neatly placed out on the yard covered with a tarp. It seemed that it was his turn to be helped."

"That next morning several big trucks and cars showed up at Bob's farm, filled with lumber, men and equipment. They dug out and formed up a new foundation and then the cement trucks came and poured the slab. In the following couple of days Bob had a brand new building. When Bob went to pay the contractor he was told that it was already paid for."

"For as long as I had known Bob he had never asked for anything. I could tell, right then that he was destined for something good. It does not happen often, usually once in your lifetime, you meet someone that is truly good.

That is the man you have for a son-in-law. So now Gheron, to answer your question; if I had thought for just one minute that there was going to be any trouble or that you would have been harmed, believe me, I would have stepped in immediately."

Gheron was speechless. It took him a few minutes to recover and collect himself.

"Bob never told me a thing about that," Gheron finally said.

"That too doesn't surprise me one bit," William said. "Bob's not the type to boast. He will give you anything and not ask for anything in return."

"Yes I know, for I have learned that personally," Gheron said. "Bob had no idea who we were or what our intentions might have been when we crashed on his farm that night. With little to no regards as to what would happen to him if he were to be found out, he jumped right in and took care of us. The Berillion race had only been observing Earth for a few centuries by then and all we had seen was fighting. I never knew humans could be so caring. That is until I met Bob."

"True, however the Vergonians have been observing Earth for quite a bit longer," William said. "And from time to time a human would come along and make a difference. No matter how small it was it gave us hope and a reason to continue watching them"

"True," Gheron said. "After I had met Bob I knew too that there was hope for Earth and those humans. That is why after talking with Bob and getting to know him, I have chosen to place them first on my League charter."

Gheron handed William the copy of The League of United Planets charter with Earth first and the names of the first ten systems listed underneath. William took the computer tablet and studied it for a few seconds.

"No, you must not mention Earth at this time," he said. "Any of the systems that do not already know about Earth must not be told, at least not yet. We must keep Earths name off the charter for now. We will simply amend the charter for now and exclude Earth. Ten worlds will give the League a good start. We will work hard and add new worlds and in time when Earth is ready, we will contact them and hopefully we will be able to make their name to the League charter, official."

William then placed the computer tablet in a drawer in his desk and after the two of them had eaten lunch William took Gheron on a tour of the city.

CHAPTER
FOUR

Several months later, with the Ambassadors all back on Pogh, they settled into a routine. They worked on forming a unified defense force, which they called 'Space Fleet', and built ships and trained officers and crews to fly them. Each member world was asked to agree to provide a certain percentage of volunteers, based on population, and have them commit to a minimum of three years of service for enlisted personnel and six years for officers.

They had scientists, doctors, engineers and all other trades represented and they were spread throughout the charter worlds. Their infrastructures were boosted and all brought up to roughly the same level. This process took about fifty years and during this time the Ambassadors themselves or their assigned delegates would go out and contact other worlds and ask them to join. Soon there were hundreds of planets in their new League.

Gheron and William became very close friends and they often sat and reminisced about Bob and wondered how he was getting along. From time to time they would hear stories about him from some of the outer systems. And it seemed that wherever he had been, he had made some sort of impression and it seemed that his presence was enough to influence the leaders of those planets and when formally contacted by the League they would be eager to sign on.

It would appear that Bob had become quite the Ambassador in his own rights. Maybe not on purpose or maybe by some greater design, but either way it would seem that he had made an impression wherever he went.

"Hello William. Are you busy?" Gheron asked one morning as he met him in the hall of the council building. "I am never to busy for you my friend," William answered. "How can I help you?"

"Did Bob ever tell you about meeting my race?" Gheron asked.

"No he did not," William answered. "I tried to see if I could get him to open up. Sometimes we would be out fishing after dark and I would ask him if he believed that there was life on other worlds. He would simply say that to think otherwise was ignorant. I asked him what he would do if he ever met an alien being and he said that he would try to make friends with them. As much as I tried to get him to tell me something, he just would not say anything. I guess he did not feel that he could trust other human beings with his secret."

"But you're not human," Gheron stated.

"No I am not. But Bob did not know that either," William said. "One thing I do know is that if you were a friend of his, he would do anything to help you, and if need be, even protect you. And if that meant keeping quiet, then that is what he did."

"Well I can tell you William, he talked about you all the time," Gheron said. "He was always telling me about his good friend Bill the sheriffs deputy and how he hated to deceive you the way he did. He told me that he wished he could have confided in you and told you everything."

"Thank you Gheron," William said. "I appreciate that, I really do."

"I understand the part about Bob wanting to help and protect his friends too," Gheron said. "When we brought Bob to Berillion to honor him, we did not think that he would ever be involved in fighting a battle, not only for his life but, for the lives of billions of people he didn't even know. Even though it was not his fight-to-fight, he insisted on it. We tried to force him to leave, even put him on a ship. But he used Leah's ship the Arrgott to escape, so we decided if he was that determined to stay and help, then we would allow him to. So we asked him to ferry supplies to the fighting ships that were involved in the low orbit defense."

"All to soon it became evident that we were outmatched and when we ordered the evacuation of Berillion, Bob took twenty-five Berillions with him in his ship, and met up with some transports, and then he led them all to Earth where they took on supplies and then most of them left."

"I know," William said. "I was informed of their imminent arrival and I was told to keep an eye on Bob and those Berillions that had decided to stay on Earth and I secretly did my part to help them whenever and wherever I could."

"Yes," Gheron said. "Bob told me that you helped him with a female named Abby when she came looking for him to help her leave the planet. He was not too sure how you were going to react when he told you that he knew her and that he would vouch for her. Bob had told me that he hoped you would probably think that he and Abby were more than just friends and he just left it at that."

"Well, I did sort of give Bob that impression," William said. "I could not very well come out and tell him that I knew Abby was a Berillion and that she needed a lift off of the planet."

"I suppose not," Gheron said and then chuckled. The two of them chatted for a while longer before Gheron excused himself and then headed off to do some work.

CHAPTER FIVE

Another fifty years or so had passed by now and The League of United Planets High Council was receiving three to four requests for admission a month from the many worlds of the outer systems. The High Council would send delegates out to these worlds to meet with their leaders and to see if they met the criteria for admission. If they did then they were allowed to join, if they did not then they were given a copy of the criteria and if they changed their ways then they could be reconsidered at a later date.

Another fifty years or so later and the League had grown rapidly. There were approximately four thousand world members now. One day the council received a request for admission from a world called Zephyr, far out in the Lotus system in the "J" sector of their Alpha quadrant. The admissions secretary called Gheron in to look at this one personally. When Gheron looked over the application he could not believe what he saw. He called in William and asked him to take a look. After William had finished he looked up at Gheron and started nodding his head.

"Did you see it?" Gheron asked excitedly. "Yes I did," William answered.

"Then I wasn't seeing things," he said. "That was Roberts name right?"

"Yes, it would seem so," William said. "We must leave at once."

Gheron and William boarded the Space Fleet's newest flagship, the U.S.S. Chevron, and headed out into space. It was a top of the line ship. It had its own shuttle bay that could hold up to three shuttle craft. It had the latest in defensive weapons and energy shields, a full medical facility and it carried a crew of over five hundred with extra accommodations for up to one hundred guests and it could travel at light speed five. But even at that, the trip out would take nearly three years.

About midway into the journey they were crossing through a desolate region of space when suddenly two very menacing warships appeared in front of them. They were hailed by the lead ship's Commander Gorch, and asked to identify themselves and state their reason for crossing into their space.

"I am Captain Bonn Elle of the U.S.S. Chevron," the Captain answered. "This is a League of United Planets vessel and we are on a diplomatic mission. We apologize for the intrusion. We were unaware that this area of space had been claimed by another race."

"This region belongs to the Andromidan Empire and you are intruding," Commander Gorch stated. "You will leave at once or be destroyed. You have five minutes to comply."

"Our mission is very important," Bonn Elle said. "Is there any way we can get your permission to pass through your space?"

"What is the nature of your business?" Commander Gorch demanded.

"As I said," Bonn Elle answered. "We are on a diplomatic mission to talk to the leader of a planet near this sector."

"I think that you are here so that you can spy on the Empire for your League of Planets." Gorch stated.

"We have no intentions of spying on your Empire," Bonn Elle said. "We have all that we need within the League."

"Then why do you seek more worlds?" Gorch asked. "I believe that you are trying to surround the Empire and attempt to take over," Gorch stated.

Commander Gorch ordered his ships to arm their weapons and target the Chevron.

"Please, there is no need for violence," Captain Bonn Elle said. "We are on a peaceful, diplomatic mission and we were asked to come and speak to the leader of a world in this sector. They want to join us; we are not trying to surround your system. We certainly do not want to surround your Empire or start a war with you."

"It is to late now, your ship will be destroyed unless you surrender immediately." Gorch stated.

"Sir, our preliminary scans of the alien vessels indicate that their weapons would do very little damage to the Chevron," the tactical officer stated.

"I will be willing to bet that they know this and are attempting to take the Chevron by bluffing and then steal our technology," the first officer added. "Or else they would have fired upon us by now."

"Good call Commander," William said as he and Gheron stepped onto the bridge. "Open the channel, I want to speak to their Commander."

"Channel open Ambassador," the communications officer said.

"I am Ambassador William Mont, from the planet Vergon in the Pegasus system and this is Ambassador Gheron from Berillion in the Gemini system," he said. "Perhaps you have heard of us. We could easily destroy both your ships before you could scratch the paint on ours.

Are you prepared to die for nothing?" There was silence for several minutes. "Well, I am waiting," William said.

"We will leave you for now," Commander Gorch said. "But be warned, you have not heard the last of the Andromidans. You may not escape so easily the next time we meet."

"I will be looking forward to that meeting Commander," William said as the two alien vessels turned and flew away at top speed.

"Captain, please resume our course for Zephyr," William said as he and Gheron left the bridge.

The Captain kept a watchful eye open for the remainder of the trip but there was no more trouble.

When they finally arrived at Zephyr they were contacted by the Prime Minister, Lola, and given the coordinates for beaming down.

Both Gheron and William met with Lola in her chambers.

"So, Ambassador Gheron, you are the creator of the League of United Planets?" Lola asked.

"No, not entirely," Gheron answered truthfully.

"Not entirely, hmm. Perhaps you are then, Ambassador William?" Lola asked as she turned towards him.

"No, I am not the creator of the League of United Planets either," William said. "But we believe you have already met him. And that is why we are here today."

"Please explain," Lola said her interest piqued. "About four years ago we believe you met a human from Earth," Gheron said. "His name is Robert Larson. He is my son-in-law, and he is the true creator of the League of United Planets in the sense that it was his idea and vision that there be some kind of unification of all the known systems in our quadrant. I took that idea and his vision and worked with many of the planets in and around our sector and persuaded them to sign up. Bob's idea has now grown into the wonderful League that we currently have today. The very same League you have asked to join."

"Does your High Council always make it a point to send their two oldest and most respected Ambassadors?" She asked.

"No," William answered this time. "Certain circumstances dictated that we come personally. You see Robert is my friend as well. And as previously mentioned, he is Ambassador Gheron's son-in-law. That is why we have come here personally to talk with you. We were hoping that he might still be here, for we would very much like to see him and talk to him again."

"I am sorry," Lola said. "He is not here, he left about two years ago. But I will tell you this he spoke very highly of you Gheron. We have been hearing stories about a League of Planets taking shape in this quadrant. We had never heard of Earth or saw a human before him. We initially thought that he might be a spy for the Andromidans."

"When we asked him about the League of United Planets he said that he did not know anything about that and then he told us to contact a Gheron on the planet Pogh and talk to him. And then he signed his name and said that we could use it so that we would have proof that we were being truthful."

"When we made contact we were told that there was indeed a League of United Planets. And then we were informed that you were coming in person that is when we knew that the rumors/stories about the League were true. And if it were true what this human was saying about being a friend of yours, well then what he was telling us about him not being a spy had to be the truth as well."

"Yes it is true. And it is a shame that we missed him too," Gheron said. "But we are here now. So, please tell us, what does Zephyr have to offer The League of United Planets then?"

"Yes of course. We have great knowledge of this sector of the galaxy," she said. "We know the boarders that exist between Andromidan space, our space and Warlon space. And we know the safe routes of travel around them."

"Yes, we have met the Andromidans," William said. "They are very suspicious of everything and warlike.

Please tell us, what are your defenses?"

"We have thousands of space ships that are equal in strength to the Andromidans. As long as we do not stray into their space they leave us alone. We have dealings with no less than six other worlds in this sector; and most of them are very nearly equal to us in technology. They also have space ships and one of the reasons that the Andromidans have not tried to invade and conquer us is because we have made a loose alliance with these worlds."

"Would it be possible to get them to agree to formalized talks?" Gheron asked.

"They are suspicious of outsiders," Lola said. "But I am certain that if we were to approach them together, we could convince them that a permanent alliance would be beneficial to all."

"What do you have for industry?" William asked.

"We have technology in power production." Lola said.

"We have developed low cost, high output power plants that produce absolutely no harmful emissions. We have knowledge of all known diseases in this sector and we have the cures for them as well."

"What do you have for agriculture?" Gheron asked.

"We have limited resources there," she said. "But what we lack there, we trade for with Phurgus, they are only a few days flight from here, they have an abundance of agriculture. We help them with the construction of power plants and with hospitals and medical supplies and they give us food supplies and help us with what little we can produce on our own. It has served us well for two centuries now."

"Will you come with Ambassador William and me to Phurgus so that we may invite them to join the League?"

"Yes, it will be an honor to stand beside Robert's friends in negotiations," Lola said.

William sensed that there was something that Lola was not telling them about Robert's visit but he put it aside for now. He was just glad for the chance that they might have two more additions to the League this far out from Pogh and their home sector.

CHAPTER
SIX

Gheron and William along with Lola signed Phurgus on to the League and Phurgus was eager to have new allies as well. With the addition of these two worlds and their knowledge of the boarder lines claimed by the Andromidans and Warlons, the League ships could now travel safely between these sectors.

Gheron contacted Pogh and had them start sending assets to this sector at once.

Lola went back to Zephyr and sent their newly elected ambassador Breen to Phurgus.

Phurgus's prime minister, Turoc assigned Gabriella as their new ambassador. They gave themselves some time to get acquainted and then they started contacting the other four worlds in this sector.

From Phurgus they went to Kath, where they met Navix, the president. It took almost a year to convince him and the planet's council that this alliance would be beneficial to them all.

Once signed on president Navix introduced them to the new ambassador for Kath, Belzar, and within a month they were on their way to the next world Perth, where they met Gavin, its president.

Of the four remaining worlds left to contact, Perth would prove to be the most difficult and time consuming to convince.

Gheron and William were the outsiders here so they would coach Gabriella, Belzar and Breen on how to be convincing and diplomatic at the same time. Kurtz, its prime minister, was old and wise and also a bit distrustful of the outsiders. He and the council studied every word and sentence in the charter. If there was some concern over just one word, it meant months of clarification and often involved actually contacting many of the worlds involved for candid and frank questioning. He and the council wanted to make absolutely sure that these planets were speaking freely, uninhibited and without coercion.

Breen and Belzar would sometimes become frustrated and aggravated by Perth's slow acceptance during the negotiations, but Gabriella had a calming charm and along with Gheron and William they showed them how to have patience and compassion. At one point Kurtz accused William of trying to take advantage of Zephyr, and that he had forced them into signing onto the League by angering the Andromidans when they crossed into their space.

William calmly explained to him that they knew absolutely nothing about the fragile, if not nonexistent, peace agreement that these worlds had with the Andromidans when they first had contact with them.

William told Kurtz that during the altercation no mention, by name, was ever given as to where they were traveling to and to whom they were meeting with.

Then Gheron spoke up, "Mr. prime minister," he said. "If our presence in this sector causes in any way, any harm to come to your world from the Andromidans you can be assured that we will stand with you and help your people drive them back without any compensation on your part. If after this you are still uninterested in joining then we will leave you in peace and continue on to the next worlds on our journey."

"The Andromidans have always left us alone," Kurtz said. "I fear that if we sign this alliance then they might think that we would become a threat to their way of lifestyle. And that in itself might provoke and attack." "Rest assured sir," William said. "If that were to happen then the full force of the League of United Planets would come to bear against the Andromidans. But I have a pretty good feeling that the Andromidans have heard of my race as well as Gheron's and I do not think that they are spoiling for an altercation just yet."

"I believe that your world will be just as safe in the future as it is right now. We will not push you into signing or doing anything that you are not comfortable with. We are willing to stay and wait patiently for your decision."

That decision finally came after nearly two years of deliberations by the leaders of Perth. When the day came for the delegation to leave Perth, Prime Minister Kurtz thanked them for staying the distance.

"We were fully aware of the fact that you have more worlds to contact," Kurtz said. "I know you could have left Perth and gone to those other worlds and left us to deliberate on our own. But you chose to stay and see it through to signing. That shows me that you are truly concerned about the planets that join and that you will stand by every word in the charter."

"Thank you sir," Gheron said. "It was a pleasure to be here and yes we will stand by every word. That you can be sure of."

And with that William, Gheron, Breen, Gabriella, Belzar and Reginald, the ambassador from Perth, left for the planets Archimedes, Algernon and Prometheus.

Archimedes was a technological dream world. Almost every aspect of daily living had some form of mechanical assistance. They had advanced computerized replicating machines for the home or space ship that could produce anything from clothing to food and drink. They had androids with artificial intelligence. These androids would work along side people in just about every job.

Their hospitals had medical equipment that could mend broken bones in hours instead of weeks. For recreation they had rooms that could project holographic images on the walls, ceiling and floor to simulate any environment from oceans to mountains and everything in between.

Money had become virtually obsolete on Archimedes, people would work and earn credits, which were then banked and when they needed to purchase something all that was required was a scan of the thumb.

The delegates met with their leader, Thomas.

"It would appear that Archimedes has much to offer The League of United Planets," Thomas said. "What do you bring to the table?"

"Yes you do have a lot to offer," William said. "And to be quite honest, I feel that we might be wasting your time by asking for this alliance. It looks like your world has more than enough resources to properly defend itself against almost any threat."

"I appreciate your honesty," Thomas said. "Don't be so eager to sell yourselves short. I see a lot of good ideas here. You have certainly put a lot of thought and effort into this alliance and I believe that we would be foolhardy to ignore such an opportunity to ally ourselves with your League. I believe it to be only a mere formality to bring this to the High Command, but I am certain we will sign with you. Please be my guests and I will get back to you as quickly as I can."

"Thank you Mr. Chairman," William said. "We appreciate your hospitality."

The delegates took their leave and headed to the quarters provided for them. The next day some of the delegates were touring the hospitals and manufacturing facilities while Gheron made a call back to Pogh. President Morrow told Gheron that the Andromidans had contacted the League council and told them that they did not like them snooping around their space. Morrow said that the Emperor informed them that they were formally charging them with espionage. Any League ship caught traveling in or near their territories would be captured or destroyed immediately. Gheron thanked President Morrow for the information and then he called the delegates back to the hotel and told them what had happened.

They were discussing their options when Chairman Thomas visited them.

"We have signed your alliance ambassador William," he said. "The entire High Command was in agreement."

"Thank you sir," William said. "But I am afraid I have received a bit of bad news from the League Council back on Pogh."

"I am sorry to hear that," Thomas said. "Is there anything I can do for you?"

"You have done enough just by signing on," William said. "But I am afraid now that you hear what I am about to say you may want to rethink your decision."

"I am sure that you are making this sound worse then it really is," Thomas said.

"We will see," William said. "I have just been informed that the Andromidans have all but declared war on The League of United Planets. We told you that we had an incident with two of their warships when we first arrived in this sector."

"Yes you did," Thomas said. "And I appreciate your telling us up front. Knowing this did not alter our Commands choice either. We have had contact with the Andromidans in the past as well and we had to quickly put them in their place. We have learned though that when pressed by an equal force they are more inclined to back down then risk loosing the challenge. What did they have to say to you?"

"We have been told that any League ship caught flying to close to Andromidan space will be captured or destroyed," William said. "I fear that we have put your people and your ships in jeopardy now that you have decided to become a member."

"Nonsense," Thomas said. "I appreciate your concern, but we can handle the Andromidans. Do not worry about our people or our ships. When it is time for you to return to your home sector we, along with the other worlds in this sector that have signed on so far, will help escort your ship through and see that no harm comes to you."

"Thank you Mr. Chairman," William said. "We appreciate the support that you are so willing to offer after only just becoming members of The League of United Planets."

"Do not give it another thought." Thomas said. "We fully understood all of the ramifications that came with signing this alliance with The League of United Planets. I heard that you were going to go to Algernon and Prometheus from here so I took the liberty of contacting their world leaders and sending them copies of the League Charter, they are both willing to join."

"Well. I don't know what to say," Gheron said. "Thank you doesn't seem quite adequate. But thank you very much Mr. Chairman."

"You are most welcome," Thomas said. "They are sending representatives here to go over some of the details. But they have both been given the authorization to formally sign the agreement; they should be here within the month. You are most welcome to stay at my home while you wait."

"Thank you again," Gheron said. "We wouldn't dream of such an imposition so I think that we should stay at the hotel. Perhaps you would allow our crew to take some shore leave while we wait."

"By all means," Thomas said. "They are more than welcome to come and enjoy our hospitality."

"Thank you, I will contact the Captain and let him know," Gheron said as Thomas left.

Gheron and William excused themselves and contacted Captain Bonn Elle and told him that the crew was welcome to take shore leave while they waited for the representatives from Algernon and Prometheus to arrive.

CHAPTER SEVEN

The representative from Algernon arrived first. Her name was Cheryl and Gheron asked her if she had any questions for them from her worlds' leaders. She told them that they had studied the charter in detail after Thomas had sent it to them and that there were just a few items she needed clarification on.

"This point on agreeing to send a percentage of the population for your Space Fleet," she started. "Is that written in stone or is it negotiable?"

"No it is not written in stone, it can be negotiated on. For the most part it has not proven to be a problem with any of the other worlds that have signed on so far," Gheron explained. "Why? Do you have a reason why we should amend it?"

"Yes we do. You see we are a nonviolent race. We have been for the past one thousand years now," Cheryl explained. "We have no intentions of going back on our beliefs."

"And you would not have to," William said. "Our Space Fleet was set up for defensive purposes only. But we are not so naive as to think that there could not be a chance that we may have to fire the first shot in order to prevent a war. Your people that agree to volunteer would not be assigned to any combat related vessels."

"What other type of vessel would you build, if it were not for the defense of The League of United Planets systems that have signed on?" Cheryl asked.

"We have built many ships that are strictly used for scientific research, exploration and first contact. They have been equipped with the most advanced defensive shields and the fastest engines that we have. They do not carry weapons, they rely on their speed and shielding to get them out of harms way. But in the event of an attack some defensive ships would be sent to assist. Your citizens would be stationed on these exploration vessels in scientific and medical positions or on Star Bases. If that is agreeable to you."

"Yes, I believe that we could agree to those conditions," Cheryl said.

"You mentioned that you had a few items that needed to be cleared up," William said. "What other areas of the charter did you have concerns with?"

"Some of the members of the World Council had concerns about cultural beliefs," Cheryl said.

"How so?" William asked.

"They did not see anywhere in the charter where safeguards and protections were set up in reference to cultural ways of life." she said. "They thought that this could lead to some form of homogenization or dilution of a member worlds culture. Or to perhaps try and make the League worlds conform to a unified culture or belief system."

"Well, I can assure you, and your world, that your cultural beliefs will in no way be infringed upon," William said. "This was an oversight on our part and was not done intentionally. We have well over four thousand worlds in The League of

United Planets now and not one member world has ever had an issue with the wording. And I can assure you that no planet has so far ever been forced to, or told that they had to, conform to any one way of lifestyle or stop the ones that they are currently following. I want to thank you for bringing this oversight to our attention and it will be addressed here and now so that now and in the future there can be no doubts as to what is asked of the member worlds."

"Thank you Ambassador William," Cheryl said. "I will inform my leaders that these concerns have been dealt with to my satisfaction and that we can go ahead and sign the charter. I will be in touch with you later to formalize the charter."

"Thank you," Gheron said. "We will be seeing you then."

Cheryl left to contact her world and let them know that their concerns had been taken care of.

A few days later the representative from Prometheus arrived, his name was Gabe and he had a copy of the signed charter with him.

"Welcome Gabe," Gheron said. "My name is Gheron and I am the ambassador from Berillion. This is ambassador William and he is from Vergon."

"Thank you ambassador Gheron, ambassador William.

I would just like to say on behalf of Prometheus that we are grateful for this opportunity to join you and the other worlds in signing this League of United Planets agreement," Gabe said. "We look forward to working with you in promoting and protecting all that you have worked for in the past and in the future to come."

"We appreciate that and we welcome you and your world to The League of United Planets," Gheron said. "Do you have any questions or concerns that you would like to discuss at this time?"

"No, our officials back on Prometheus have gone over the documents with a fine tooth comb and all is in order. And if it is all the same to you and the others I believe we should probably get ready to go to Pogh as soon as possible to get settled in."

"Yes," Gheron said. "We are ready to leave just as soon as ambassador Cheryl gets the OK from her world officials."

Later that day Cheryl arrived and told the delegates that all was ready and after a good meal and a full nights rest, they departed on the journey back to Pogh. They made a short pit stop on Zephyr to thank Lola once again for all the help that she had given them in finding new worlds to sign on and also to check in with the newly formed Space Fleet ships that had flown out with supplies and information about the many member worlds that have already signed on.

Captain Bonn Elle contacted the Captain of the research vessel Sheridan to find out how the trip out had been. He was informed that they had a slight altercation with an Andromidan scout ship but one of the Archimedes battle ships had come out to escort them in and when the Andromidans saw it they immediately left the area. After a brief stay they continued on the long journey to Pogh.

Half way into the trip back to Pogh the crew and delegates on the Chevron found themselves being pursued by four Andromidan warships. The Andromidans were well outside their proposed boarder line so the Captain of the Chevron ordered the helmsman to maintain course and speed and ignore the pursuing vessels. The Commander of the lead ship hailed the Chevron several times but Captain Bonn Elle told his communications officer to ignore him. This infuriated the Andromidans and they attempted to stop the Chevron by firing their weapons across its bow.

At this point, Captain Bonn Elle contacted the lead vessels Commander Tuck, and reminded him that they had left the protection of Andromidan space and were now violating free space and that if they did not turn back he would be forced to return fire and then report their actions to the League.

Commander Tuck of the lead ship Pommel, informed the Captain of the Chevron that he was well within his rites to stop them because they were being charged with espionage. And by this reasoning alone he could shoot the Chevron down. Bon Elle ordered his tactical officer to target the lead ships weapons and shield generators and fire when he gave the order.

"Commander Tuck," he said. "As you probably can tell, we have targeted your weapons and shields. If you do not turn back now, we will be forced to fire."

"I do not think you will want to risk a war by doing that," Commander Tuck stated. "I strongly advise you to surrender, now."

"It is you who are risking a war by trying to detain us," Bonn Elle said.

"The time for talk is over," Commander Tuck said and then he ordered his weapons officer to fire on the Chevron.

"Direct hit Commander, no effect," he said. "Return fire, now," Captain Bonn Elle ordered. "Direct hit sir, their ship is disabled," the tactical officer replied.

"Turn back now, Commander Tuck," Bonn Elle ordered over the radio. "Or the next round destroys your ship."

Commander Tuck gave the order for the other ships to attack and they fired their weapons at the Chevron with little to no effect.

"I want you to target the other three ships weapons generators and fire on my command," Captain Bonn Elle ordered.

"Ready," replied the tactical officer.

"This is the Captain of the Chevron," Bonn Elle said on an open hail. "If you do not want to suffer the same fate as Commander Tuck, I suggest you also turn back now."

One of the Andromidan ships fired again, still with no effect.

"Fire," ordered the captain.

The Chevron's weapons cut through the Andromidans shields and took out their weapons.

"Again, turn back now or be destroyed," Bonn Elle said.

"You will pay dearly for this Captain Bonn Elle," Tuck said as he turned his ship to ram the Chevron.

"Evasive maneuvers," the Captain ordered. "Target their engines, let's take the fight out of these guys."

"Weapons ready sir," the tactical officer replied. "Fire," Bonn Elle ordered.

"Direct hit, their engines are now off-line, the Pommel is dead in space and drifting sir," the tactical officer responded.

With the ship now disabled, Captain Bonn Elle was about to contact its Commander when it suddenly blew up.

"What happened?" Bonn Elle asked. "I said to target their engines only..."

"He self-destructed their ship Captain," William said as he stepped onto the bridge. "It is common practice for these warrior type races to kill themselves rather than be captured."

With the destruction of the leader the other three ships turned and flew off at light speed. Captain Bonn Elle resumed his course for Pogh and ordered full speed ahead and then he contacted Space Fleet Command and advised them of the situation. The rest of the trip went off without a hitch.

CHAPTER
EIGHT

Some years later while on Pogh, William Mont received a priority message from his home world Vergon. He immediately called Gheron in for a sit down and a few weeks later they were on route to Earth from Pogh. Within a year they were entering the Sol system. They made radio contact with the world defense headquarters in order to set up a meeting. When the Earth government received the radio message they were shocked and somewhat surprised and they immediately went into a defensive mode. The world defense military leader, general Michaels sent out several battle ships into orbit with a message requesting immediate identification and the reason why they had entered into Earth's space.

"My name is Gheron," he said. "There is no need for violence, we have come in peace. I am an ambassador with The League of United Planets. It is too much to try to explain at the moment. But now that you have finally developed your faster than light speed engines we feel that now would be a good time to contact your government and attempt to explain just what that will mean for the people of your planet. We wish to set up a meeting with your world leader in order to give him/her the necessary information needed to prepare for what now lies ahead of you. Will you allow us to land so that we can talk?"

"I will have to clear it with the government," General Michaels said. "You will remain in orbit until we contact you in this regard."

"Understood," Gheron replied. "We eagerly await your decision."

William and Gheron patiently waited for two weeks.

Finally they were told that they could come down. The two of them boarded a shuttle and instructed the pilot to launch. One of the military ships escorted them down to a secure military installation far from any populated cities. When they landed their shuttle, several armed military soldiers surrounded it; then a couple of them searched William and Gheron, taking their files and handing them to General Michaels. Then General Michaels escorted Gheron and William into a large hangar that had been turned into a make shift conference room for the occasion. Under heavy guard the leader of Earths government was escorted into the hangar and stood across the table from Gheron and William.

"Welcome to Earth, I am World President Charles Faulkner," he said as he shook each of their hands. "Please have a seat, I apologize for all the security but you must understand that you are the first aliens to officially make contact with us. So, who are you and what is this League of United Planets that you spoke of?"

"We understand about security completely," William said first. "My name is William Mont I am the Ambassador from a planet called Vergon and this is Ambassador Gheron originally from a planet called Berillion and currently the planet Pogh. Our job is to make contact with emerging worlds/civilizations like Earth. We have brought with us the files explaining The League of United Planets in greater detail, what it is and what it can mean for the people of Earth. We will try to answer any questions you might have and to explain why we have chosen this time to come here."

"Why would we need your help?" Charles asked. Gheron and William looked at each other and smiled.

"Mr. president," William said. "Now that your race has developed light speed capabilities yours has now been classified as an "emerging race". We have come here to welcome you into a new era but more importantly, we have come here to let you know that you are not alone in this galaxy anymore and ask that you let us guide you and protect you on this new and exciting journey…"

"We have weapons to defend ourselves with and we can travel at light speed now," president Faulkner said. "I'm sure we would do just fine out there."

"Maybe," William stated next. "We could just leave and let you go out into the vast unknown, naked, but you would find out in a hurry that the galaxy you call home can be a deadly place to explore. But that would serve no pertinent purpose. In this sector alone there are no less than one hundred inhabited planets that have been using faster than light speed travel for centuries now and they would not appreciate your armed vessels coming out and confronting them."

"Right now you are young and arrogant and feeling quite smug about your achievements. But if you went out there and tried to bully your way around, your ships would be destroyed before you could get off one shot. The shuttle craft. that we have arrived in is faster and has more shielding and firepower then your newly constructed battle ships have. We will tell you this much for now, President Faulkner, most all of the planets in this sector are League of United Planets members; signed to assist and defend one another..."

"Ha, you're just trying to scare us away," president Faulkner said. "You don't want us to explore on our own."

"That is not true," William said. "We are just trying to tell you that we know what lies ahead of you and if that scares you a little then maybe you understand that what we are saying holds some truth. However, you are certainly free to decide not to join and that will be fine as well, we would be disappointed but we would respect your decision. You can go and explore space on your own and make contact with any of these planets. But they will not help you gain technology and they will defend their right to keep that technology private."

"Currently less than a dozen worlds in this sector know that you exist out here and Ambassador Gheron and I come from two of these worlds. We have deliberately kept Earth off the radar. Like it or not, my race has been monitoring your evolution for many millennia now. And now that you have "arrived" so to speak we feel that you are ready to take this next step. We know that your race will become a great asset to the League and become a powerful influence for all the planets of the League."

"How could you possibly know that?" Charles asked. "Like Ambassador William just said," Gheron now spoke. "The Vergons have been watching your world for a very long time now. A few other races like mine from Berillion not as long and we have seen your race at its very worst and we have seen, also, your human capacity for compassion and loyalty. That is how we know."

"Please, please take the files, study them, take your time and review them thoroughly. More importantly, use our knowledge and experience; ask us all the questions you want. We will be honest and forthright and in the end if you still choose to be left alone, rest assured you will be. But if you decide to join; then you would have access to advanced technologies beyond your expectations." "Thank you both, you have certainly opened our eyes,"

Charles said. "You have given us a lot of information to digest. It will take us some time to study all of it. You are welcome to stay here if you want. We have prepared quarters for you nearby."

"We appreciate that," William said. "But we think that it will be less stressful for you and your military if we return to our ship. You can contact us at any time and we can beam down and answer any of your questions and alleviate any of your concerns."

"Beam down? What do you mean by that?" Charles asked.

"We have a device that turns matter into energy and then sends that energy to any location and then turns the energy back into matter," Gheron explained. "Just one more piece of technology that you will have access to if and when you decide to join."

"Sounds very interesting. OK then, I'm sure that I will be calling on you," Charles said as he shook their hands and walked out.

William and Gheron went back to the ship and for the next six months they answered questions and, for the first time, allowed some of the military officials to tour their ship. It took some time but the government of Earth did finally sign with the League and now their name could be officially added to The League of United Planets roster.

For most all of its history, the people of Earth had always thought that they were alone, at least in this part of the galaxy, so special care had to be used to ease Earth into the mix. And in time Earth was introduced to all of the member races of the League and soon they started to blossom.

Now for the first time the citizens of Earth could travel out into space. Before now only a select few were ever given the opportunity to travel beyond the pull of its gravity. And so the people of Earth poured their hearts and souls into the League and within ten years you would have never known that they had just signed on. The citizens of Earth were eager to get out and explore their newfound universe.

One day, several more years later, the new president of Earth, Karl Svenson, called William and asked to see him. "Thank you for seeing me Mr. ambassador," Karl said.

"It is always an honor Mr. president. How can I help you?" William asked.

"Please don't take this the wrong way," he started. "But I have been looking over the League charter and I have a couple of questions that I would like answered."

"That is perfectly Okay," William said. "The League charter is a living charter and it grows and adapts with the addition of every new world. We cherish any thoughts and input from any member planet. What are your questions or concerns?"

"When you first came here and made contact with my predecessor, you said that your people had been watching our development for many centuries," Karl stated. "In all that time have you ever tried to alter the way we did things?"

"No! The Vergonian race has a non-interference policy that we have lived by for many millennia," William said. "We would never interfere with the development of any planet now. We learned a very valuable lesson about fifteen thousand years ago. We were watching a planet that we knew had great potential and contact was made and suffice it to say it nearly destroyed the planet. So after that we have just watched and hoped that those worlds would grow and prosper on their own."

"How about the other races in the galaxy? Do they have a non-interference policy as well?" Karl asked.

"As far as I know, only a handful of races feel the way we do," William replied. "Is that a concern of yours?"

"A minor one. Far be it from me to tell you how to run the League, but I think that there should be a similar policy written in so that the member planets would not be tempted to try to speed up the development of any race it might come into contact with. I think it should be a number one rule," Karl said.

"You make a very good point," William said. "I believe we should bring that up with the League High Council immediately. See, I knew Earth would become a valuable asset to the League. You said that you had more questions?"

"Yes. I also did not see anything in here that addresses what the League can or cannot do for a member world if it should have internal conflicts within its own government. What are your thoughts on that issue?"

"Another very good question," William said. "It happened not to long after the charter was started, we had only a dozen worlds signed on then. One of the planets nations had a minor border dispute. Their world leader wanted to use League ships to go in and stop the dispute. We elected to pull out and sit back until the two nations could work out their differences. Sadly, it took them five years to settle on the borders and there was some discussion on whether or not to let them back in. In time they were allowed to rejoin and now they are one of the finest races we have. Since then there has never been another problem with any member world and to tell you the truth, we simply forgot about it."

"I think there should be a written policy to address such an issue in the future," Karl said. "It might just save any future embarrassment to the League itself."

I agree," William said. "I will bring it to the Councils attention as well. Do you have anything else that you would like to see added or changed?"

"No. I believe that about covers it," Karl said. "Thank you again for seeing me. I hope I have not been a bother to you, Mr. Ambassador. I know you are probably very busy and I appreciate you taking time out of your schedule."

"Do not give it a second thought," William said. "That is what an Ambassador's job is. I want you to know that we are never too busy to answer any questions that member races might have. The only way we can grow is to have input from our members. If that is all you have then I will get this to the attention of the High Council at once."

"That is all I have," Karl said. "I hope to hear from you soon. Good day Ambassador William."

And with that, Ambassador William shook Karl's hand and left.

CHAPTER
NINE

Several years later a Space Fleet ship, the U.S.S. Patton, was conducting a search mission for a League of United Planets exploration vessel that was overdue. When the Patton strayed to close to the Warlon border they found themselves being hailed by a Warlon Battle Cruiser.

"I am Commander Dorhn of the Warlon battle cruiser Boratt. You are violating Warlon space," Dorhn stated. "What are you doing here?"

"I am Captain John Douglas of the Space Fleet vessel the U.S.S. Patton," the Captain stated. "We are searching for a League vessel that is past due. We were not aware that this area was now within your territory. Our charts still indicate that this is League space. I apologized for the intrusion, we will leave.

Commander Dorhn of the Warlon cruiser took offense and fired a warning shot across their bow.

"Stand down and prepare to be boarded," he ordered. "If you refuse you will be destroyed."

"Shields up, go to battle stations," the Captain ordered. "Hold your fire Commander Dorhn. Like I said. We are on a routine search mission for a missing League exploration vessel. Again, I apologize for coming to close to your border we meant no disrespect. We will leave immediately."

"You will do no such thing," barked Commander Dorhn. "You have violated our space and if you do not surrender your vessel it will be destroyed along with your crew."

"Is that so?" Captain Douglas replied. "Our scans indicate that we are still several million kilometers from the border of your space. It would appear that you are in fact in our space and by law, we have every right to defend ourselves. It is your ship and crew that would be destroyed, Commander. So I ask that you return to your space and leave us to our mission."

Captain Douglas turned to his communications officer and said, "Send a message to Space Fleet Command and let them know what is happening."

Commander Dorhn ordered his weapons be charged and shields set to maximum.

"Sir," the tactical officer of the Patton said. "The Boratt is charging weapons and targeting our engines. They have sent out a message for reinforcements."

"Strengthen shields in that area," Captain Douglas ordered and then he turned his attention back to the Commander of the Boratt and said, "You are risking a war with the League of United Planets if you persist in this course of action. Leave now and no harm will be done. If you refuse this request then we have no choice but to disable your vessel or destroy it."

"You will not find us so easy to destroy," Commander Dorhn said. "This ship is superior to any Space Fleet vessel you have. You will surrender your vessel or we will destroy it."

"Captain, our sensors indicate that we have the better ship," the tactical officer on the Patton stated.

"Thank you Lt.," the Captain said. "Commander Dorhn, you had better check your sensor readings again. It would appear that you are incorrect in your assumption."

Commander Dorhn ordered his weapons officer to open fire on the Patton.

"Minimal damage Commander," the weapons officer on the Boratt stated. "Their shields are holding." "Target their weapons and return fire," Captain Douglas ordered.

"Direct hit Captain, their shields and weapons are down to fifty percent," the tactical officer on the Patton stated. "It's likely their shields won't take another hit." "Get me their Commander," the Captain ordered.

"On screen Captain," the communication officer stated. "Commander Dorhn, your shields will not survive another hit," Captain Douglas stated. "I advise you to turn and leave now before it is to late."

"It is already to late," Commander Dorhn replied.

Just then another Warlon battle cruiser appeared out of nowhere and fired its weapons on the Patton.

"Shield strength is down to eighty-five percent Captain," the tactical officer advised.

"Evasive maneuvers," the Captain ordered. "Fire on their weapons now."

The Patton's weapons cut into the Warlon cruiser. "The second ship's weapons are off line," the tactical officer said.

"Target their engines and fire," ordered the captain.

But just as the Patton fired its weapons the second ship disappeared.

"Report!" The Captain ordered.

"No debris on scans sir. Our weapons must have missed when they cloaked Captain," the tactical officer replied.

Just then the Patton was hit with a second volley of weapons fire from the invisible ship.

"Calculate their trajectory and fire all weapons full spread," the Captain ordered.

The tactical officer fired once again and the ship reappeared.

"They are hit now sir," he said. "Their cloak appears to be off line."

"Good. Target their weapons and engines and fire again," the Captain ordered.

"Direct hit Captain, their ship is disabled," the tactical officer stated. "Weapons and light drive are off line. They are sending out a distress call."

"Sir, there is a message coming in from Space Fleet," the communications officer reported. "They are sending two ships and they will be here within the hour."

"Good. Give me a damage report at once," the Captain ordered.

"Our shields are down to fifty percent," the first officer reported. "One of the weapons ports on the starboard side is off line. Our light engines are off line but we still have sub-light engines, Captain."

"Plot a course for the nearest Star Base and contact the Captains of the two Space Fleet vessels," the Captain ordered. "Let them know what happened and advise them of our status."

"Aye sir," the first officer replied.

"Now get me the Commander of the Boratt," the Captain ordered.

"On screen Captain," the tactical officer reported. "Commander Dorhn, I have two League battle ships coming and they will be here in under an hour. I suggest you be gone before they get here. I have been very patient and tolerant so far but if you persist, I will have no other choice but to destroy your vessel."

"That is your problem human, you have no stomach for the kill," Commander Dorhn replied. "But I have no problem with it."

Dorhn's ship opened fire on the Patton with all the weapons it could muster but it wasn't enough to bring it down.

"Shields are down to thirty percent Captain," the first officer reported.

"Understood," the Captain replied. "Open fire."

The Patton's weapons cut through the Boratt like a hot knife through butter. The Boratt was completely destroyed. Captain Douglas now turned his attention to the second Warlon cruiser.

"Leave this space now Commander, or suffer the same fate as the Boratt," Captain Douglas said.

Suddenly there was weapons fire from the second ship. "Captain our shields are off line," the tactical officer reported. "We won't survive another attack."

"Fire all weapons," the Captain ordered. "Let's end this now!"

The Patton's weapons cut through the second Warlon battle cruiser before its Commander had time to react. The second Warlon cruiser was destroyed also. Captain Douglas ordered immediate repairs to the shields as they slowly returned to base.

The Patton had traveled for about thirty minutes when another Warlon cruiser appeared behind them.

"Captain..." the first officer started.

"I see it," Captain Douglas replied. "What's our status?"

"Forward weapons are at seventy-five percent and aft weapons are at fifty percent and charging. Port shield generator is off line, shields are only up to fifty percent. If they fire we could be seriously disabled if not destroyed," the first officer reported.

"Understood," Captain Douglas replied. "Turn the bow into them and call them."

"On screen Captain," the communications officer reported.

"You are violating League space," Captain Douglas said. "If you do not turn around now we will destroy your ship. This will be your only warning; I'm through giving second chances anymore. Close the channel."

Turning to his tactical officer he said, "Target the ship with all weapons, if they don't stop and turn around in ten seconds open fire. I've had it with these bastards."

Just then the two League ships dropped out of light speed and took defensive positions on either side of the Patton. The Warlon cruiser turned and sped away at light speed.

"This is Captain Dean Jones of the U.S.S. Justice.

What's your status Captain Douglas," he asked.

"Light speed engines are off line, shields are at sixty- five percent now and weapons are at seventy-five percent, we had to fire up a couple auxiliary power units to compensate for our damaged engines," Captain Douglas reported. "We are going to need a major overhaul."

"Understood Captain, we will escort you back to base and assist with your repairs along the way."

"Thank you Captain Jones, I appreciate the help," Captain Douglas replied.

The trip back to base was uneventful, repair teams from all three ships worked around the clock to bring on the light drive. Finally the Patton was able to jump to light speed two. The trip back to base took three weeks.

This would not be the last time the League and Warlon Empire would clash. For the next fifty years or so, there would be minor clashes and border disputes. And as always, it was up to either William or Gheron to contact the Warlon Emperor and try to negotiate some sort of peace treaty that would satisfy them all. For many years, Gheron had tried to convince the Warlon Empire to become an active member in the League of United Planets, but the Warlons were stubborn and they did not want to give up their sovereignty any time soon. The best that they could do was to agree to a shaky truce and hope that it would hold.

CHAPTER
TEN

Several years later President Gheron received a message that the new Ambassador from Zephyr would be arriving in a few days. He had her quarters made ready so that she could settle in as quickly as possible and when Lola arrived on Pogh she immediately sought out Gheron and William. She found Gheron at his home a short drive out from the capital city, however William had gone back to Vergon and was not due back for another couple of days.

"Welcome to Pogh Ambassador Lola, I'm sorry to say that William will not be back for another two days," Gheron said. "I do hope your trip in was uneventful."

"Thank you President Gheron, it was," she said. "If it is important I can have William here by morning," Gheron offered.

"No, it is not that important," she said. "I guess that I will have to talk to him when he returns then."

"So, we were surprised to hear that you stepped down as Prime Minister to take an Ambassador position," Gheron said. "What made you decide to do that?"

"Oh, I guess you can say that I would much rather be in the thick of things then sitting on the sidelines," She answered. "On that note, how do you like your position as the League's high President?"

"It is Okay," he answered. "It has only been five years now and I am finding the transition from active Ambassador to President a bit restrictive."

"Well, there you have it," she said. "That is why I chose an Ambassadorial position too."

"I see what you mean," he said as he let out a laugh.

"So then, what can I do for you?"

"Right," she started. "Well. I could sense when we first met, some twenty years ago, that you might have had some questions when I spoke about Bob's visit to our planet. I felt that I owed you and William an explanation but you never pressed the issue then so I let it slide because I thought perhaps your curiosity would get the better of you and you would eventually ask me about it. I realize that you must have very strong feelings for him, as he is your son-in-law, and I could sense that you and William were truly saddened when you learned that he was not there."

"True," Gheron stated. "William and I just figured that there had to be a good reason you kept it a secret and we have long since learned it best not to press an issue. We hoped that you would tell us someday and, look, here you are."

"Yes, here I am," she said with a laugh. "Better late than never. So I shall attempt to explain it to you. When Bob came to Zephyr we found him in his stasis pod. Our sensors had picked up a Leviathan/ship entering our system and then coming near our planet but it did not make contact. We thought that it might be a spy ship from Andromidan as we had never encountered such a creature before. It paused for only a minute and then continued on its way. A few hours later our satellites picked up an energy signature on an island in one of our oceans. There, we found Robert in his stasis pod, still in suspended animation. Along with him and his pod there was a whole lot of equipment and supplies piled nearby. Our military quickly secured the area and called in a few scientists and doctors."

"Our scientists quickly figured out how to revive him and how to open the pod. When the pod opened he sat up slowly. He looked around and when he saw the military, scientists, and doctors he asked them where he was. One of our scientists told him that he was on an island on the planet Zephyr. Then the military Commander stepped in and asked him where he had come from and if he was a spy for the Andromidans."

"He said that he most definitely was not a spy for the Andromidans and then he told them that he was from a planet called Earth. When he stood up to step out of the pod our commander saw that he was armed with a sidearm of some kind. He drew his stunner and ordered him to stay still."

"He asked Bob if he was armed and he said yes, two of them. One of the doctors started laughing and turned and walked towards Bob. The Commander told her to stop; she just turned and told him to be quiet for a minute. Then she approached him and scanned him with her medical scanner; Bob was standing there with his arms in the air. When the doctor finished her scans she reached out and gently took his arms and lowered them down to his side. The Commander ordered her to stop and get away from him but she just stood there and started asking him some questions and when she was finished he told her to take his sidearm so that there could be no mistake that he wasn't there to harm any of them."

"Then she asked him what he was doing on the island and he said that there must have been some kind of problem with his ship and that is why he was dropped off on the island. The Commander asked him where the rest of his crew was and Bob just said that he was the only crew member on his ship. He asked Bob how he could have gotten off the ship while he was in stasis and he told him that his ship, the Arrgott, was fully automated."

"Bob was then taken into custody and questioned thoroughly, all the while the doctor was nearby monitoring him. She called me and told me that Bob was not a threat and that he should be released at once…"

"That doctor must have held a very high medical position in order for her to call the Prime Minister of her planet and make such a request," Gheron stated.

"Yes, you could say that," Lola said. "You see, that doctor is my daughter, Arena, and she persisted until I had to go see Bob for myself. The military had other ideas and did not want me anywhere near him because they were not fully convinced that he was telling the truth. They still thought that he was a spy for Andromidan. The security was very tight when I arrived at the detention center where he had been sent. I met with the military Commander and he insisted that I leave and not see the prisoner. I thanked him for his concern but reminded him that I was still Prime Minister."

"I spoke with Bob for several hours and I came to the same conclusion that my daughter had. He was not a threat, and there had to be a reasonable explanation as to how and why he was there. I ordered his release into the doctor's care until we could find out what his story was. The Commander did not like it at all but he conceded with the exception that an armed guard be present at all times. I told him that that would be satisfactory and then I told my daughter to take good care of him until we could clear things up."

"A few weeks later Arena called and told me that I needed to stop by and have a chat with Bob. I dropped by over the weekend and I had a very enlightening talk with him. He told me more about his ship and how he had arrived on the island. He said that his ship was a living entity and that every so often it needed to have a really big feeding and that the Arrgott had detected a food source nearby and dropped him off to feed. And then he told me about his home world Earth, and how he met you and eventually about his lost wife and how he was searching for her."

"He had told me about the destruction of your home world and how he did his part to try and help. He told me about what he had been doing to help the other survivors of your race that had decided to stay behind on his planet. Then he told me about his friend Bill; and how he hated to have to lie to him. Then he told me that I could contact you to verify his story and if and when I did, I should use his name and that should get your attention. It did at that and more. You could imagine my surprise when I discovered that you were the one who had started this League of Planets thing that we had heard stories and rumors about back then in our sector."

"And then when you and William showed up a couple of years later, and started telling me about him, I knew he had to be more than just a friend of yours by the way you spoke about him. And it did not take me long to figure out that William was actually his friend, Bill also."

"Yes, I was shocked when I learned about that as well," Gheron said. "Imagine my surprise when I found out that my son-in-law was on a first name basis with a Vergonian. And that they had been friends for many years."

"Exactly. I took some time to study up on some of the races that have become members," Lola said. "I read about the Vergon race. It seems that they are one of the oldest known races in this part of the galaxy and one of the most secretive as well. It seemed odd to me that Ambassador William would find a friend in a person from a race of people that were considered to be to primitive for contact. He must have known something that we do not."

"True," Gheron said. "William told me how, while he was on Earth observing them, he happened to meet Bob. Then William told me that he had a sense about him; he somehow knew that he would be a part of something bigger than any of us could fully comprehend. So, what was it that Bob had done to change your mind about him?"

"I believe you could say that he stole my heart," she said. "While he was on Zephyr I fell in love with him. Oh, I thought it was just a little crush but the longer he stayed, and the more I got to know him, the more I found myself falling for him. I knew he was married because he told me but I just could not help myself. Something about him just made it so damned easy. He kept talking about Leah and how he had to keep searching for her. I just kept on finding excuses to be near him and finally one day he just gave in to me. I felt really bad because I knew how much he missed Leah but I could not control my own feelings either. He stayed as long as he could. He took on some supplies and then he said that he had to go, he said he had to search for Leah even if it took all of his lifetime."

"I understand completely," Gheron said. "William and I learned that he has never stayed more than a few years at any one place. He is driven and that is just one of the many reasons that I am proud to call him "son". I am pretty sure if you asked William he would more than likely tell you the same thing. I know a little something about the Vergon race as well. They are honest, kind and benevolent and they know more about the universe then any one can imagine. It is said that they even have command over time and space. Some have even dared to refer to them as Gods.

"I would not go so far as to say that," William said as he suddenly entered the room.

"What?...William... How...? When did you get here?" Gheron stammered.

"A few minutes ago. I let myself in, I hope I am not intruding," William said.

"No, you can never intrude," Gheron said. "But how did you know to come back, now?"

"I concluded my business early," William said. "I was informed that the new Ambassador from Zephyr was supposed to arrive today and I thought that I should be here to great her but it seems I am a bit late after all."

"Your just in time," Lola said. "How have you been Ambassador William?"

"Fine Ambassador Lola," he answered. "Have I missed anything important?"

"I was just telling Gheron how I came to know Bob," she answered.

For the next few hours the three of them sat and talked. Lola retold her story to William. She told him everything that she had told Gheron earlier. As she talked, Gheron prepared a meal. They ate and had a few drinks and then William told Lola the story of how he had met Bob for the first time on Earth. Lola sat there listening to every word and she had to turn away for a moment to wipe away the tears. William told

Lola that after that night he had a deep respect for Bob and he made it his personal mission to secretly watch over him.

They talked more about the League and how Bob had a hand in its beginnings, even if he did not know it. They sat and talked and before they knew it darkness had descended upon them and it was soon time for Lola to get to her residence.

"Thank you very much for telling me about Bob," she said. "I hope we can sit and talk some more. I should be getting back to my quarters, good night Ambassador, good night Mr. President I'll see you at the office."

"Good night Ambassador Lola," William and Gheron said to her before she left and drove away.

Gheron and William sat and chatted a bit more before William had to leave too.

CHAPTER
ELEVEN

Many years later the League research vessel U.S.S. Jordan, was traveling to rendezvous with the Coral, a ship from the planet Prometheus, to pick up some medical supplies that were needed to combat an outbreak of Algerian flue that occurred on the planet Wroth. An hour out Captain Keller from the Jordan contacted Captain Morgan from the Coral to confirm the rendezvous point.

"Captain Morgan, is there anything that I need to know about the medical supplies?" Keller asked.

"It is imperative that the serum canisters be kept in their bio-containment spheres at minus fifty degrees Celsius until they can be seeded into the atmosphere of the infected planet," Captain Morgan answered.

"Understood," Captain Keller replied. "We will have the necessary arrangements ready by the time we meet."

"Thank you Captain Keller, we should be there in less then an hour," Captain Morgan said.

"Good, I'll see you then," Captain Keller replied.

Several hours later the shuttle craft. from the Coral had just docked after returning from shuttling the last load of serum canisters to the Jordan when four Andromidan warships appeared out of nowhere and started firing their weapons on the two ships.

"What the… Evasive maneuvers, activate shields and charge weapons, and get me a damage report," Captain Keller ordered. "Where did they come from?"

"Unknown sir," the tactical officer replied. "Contact the Coral and see if they suffered any damages," Captain Keller ordered.

"The Coral reports no damage, the Captain wants to know what you intend to do," the communications officer stated.

"Red alert, raise shields and return fire, target the enemy's weapons generators," the Captain ordered. "Fire when ready!"

The Jordan's weapons flashed to life hitting one of the enemy ships knocking out its weapons. The Coral was evading and firing its weapons at two of the other Andromidan ships simultaneously. One ship exploded and the other ships weapons were disabled. The remaining ship kept firing on the Jordan knocking out its aft weapons generator.

"Return fire!" Captain Keller ordered.

Just as the Jordan's weapons fired the Andromidan ship vanished.

"Full sensor sweep, find that ship," Captain Keller ordered. "I want a full damage report as soon as possible and get me the Captain of the Coral."

"Captain Morgan for you sir," the communications officer replied.

"What's your status?" Captain Keller asked.

"Our shields are down ten percent and our port bow thruster is off line," Captain Morgan reported. "How are you?"

"Aft weapons are off line and our shields are down twenty percent," Captain Keller replied. "Can you get a sensor reading on the Andromidan ship out there?"

"Nothing yet, Captain," Morgan replied. "It would appear the Andromidans have improved their cloaking technology. I have contacted Prometheus and they are sending out four battle ships to our position. More importantly, how is the cargo?"

"The cargo is safe for now, thank you," Captain Keller replied.

Just then the Andromidan ship reappeared with another ship and they fired on the two League ships again.

"Damn it," Morgan muttered.

The Coral fired its weapons on both of the attacking ships while the Jordan concentrated its weapons on only one ship. With the combined weapons fire the ship exploded leaving only one Andromidan ship but before the Coral or Jordan could fire another volley, it disappeared once again.

They were licking their wounds and scanning for the elusive Andromidan ship while repair teams from both vessels got started. Captain Morgan contacted Prometheus and gave them an update. He was told that the four battleships were still six hours out; Captain Morgan said thanks and signed off he then contacted Captain Keller and told him what he had learned. It took a few hours and all the ships systems were back on-line. If the Jordan was to get the medical supplies delivered in time they would have to leave now. Captain Morgan agreed to escort them, he contacted Prometheus and then they headed out at full speed.

They were cruising along at top speed in order to make up the time from their delay with the Andromidans.

Everything was running smoothly and it looked like they would make it with time to spare when suddenly six Andromidan war ships de-cloaked and attacked in full force. The Coral's engines were dead and they were just floating in space and all of the Jordan's systems were off- line as well.

It didn't look good so the order was given to abandon the ships. S.O.S. beacons were launched from both ships with all the log information from the battle. The escape pods were launched and when they were well away Captain Morgan and Captain Keller gave the final order to self-destruct their ships in hopes that they would take out a few of the Andromidan ships in the process. Captain Keller used the Jordan's maneuvering thrusters to put some distance between it and the Coral in order to maximize the destructive radius and in a coordinated move, the Coral's Captain initiated the self-destruct, fifteen seconds later Captain Keller of the Jordan initiated its self-destruct.

Within five minutes the Coral disappeared in a huge ball of fire and the Jordan, fifteen seconds later suffered the same fate. The plan worked, the combined explosions took out three of the Andromidan warships. When the four Space Fleet battleships from Prometheus arrived on scene they found three Andromidan warships slightly damaged and the debris from the Jordan, the Coral and the three destroyed Andromidan warships. They took incoming fire but they were able to evade severe damage. They returned fire destroying two of the remaining warships. The third ship set course back to Andromidan and cloaked as it sped away.

The Captain of the lead League vessel immediately contacted Space Fleet and apprised them of the situation and started retrieving the escape pods as well as the S.O.S. beacons.

When the news of the attack reached Space Fleet headquarters the Admiral contacted the Andromidan Emperor and demanded an explanation. He received a reply that shook him down to the bone. The Andromidan Emperor had declared war against the League and all League worlds. Off and on for the next five to ten years the Andromidans would attack any ships that flew to close to Andromidan space. Space Fleet developed faster, stronger ships as a result of those attacks. The Andromidans would attack and destroy any outpost that they thought were being used to spy on them and it didn't matter to them if they belonged to the League of United Planets or any other race including the Warlons, they were all fair game. The Andromidans were a suspicious and paranoid race that thought everyone was out to get them and they were willing to do anything to protect their way of life and to hell with anyone who would attempt to stop them.

CHAPTER
TWELVE

The League kept signing on more and more systems and one day word filtered in to the League that the Andromidans had attacked several Warlon outposts near their two borders killing many Warlon civilians as well as some of the warriors dispatched to defend the outposts.

Gheron realized that this was a good time to try to get the Warlons back to the negotiating table. Gheron informed the Council that he was going to try to talk to the Warlon Emperor once again about joining the League. Gheron contacted the Warlon Emperor Clang, and requested an audience; it was granted. The trip out took about nine months and when Gheron arrived at the Warlon home world he sat down with Clang and they talked once again about the Warlon Empire joining up with The League of United Planets.

"Emperor Clang," Gheron said. "This alliance will greatly benefit both the Warlon Empire and the League."

"How so?" Clang asked.

"Well for one, it would free up the borders between League space and the Warlon Empire's space," Gheron said.

"The Warlon Empire does not want to give up its borders," Clang barked. "We like them the way they are."

"Okay, listen to me. First, you would not be giving up any of your borders," Gheron explained. "What this alliance would mean is that it would open them up so that our two factions could more easily travel through this sector when we go from system to system in the course of our duties. It would shave off months of travel time alone. Then there is the added benefit of security and protection for both our space vessels. We would be agreed to help your ships if they are confronted by an enemy or suffer some sort of problems and you would be agreed to assist our ships under similar circumstances. That is all; we are not trying to take the space that you have claimed as yours. We would just like to travel through your space and have peaceful coexistence between our races."

"You make good points," Clang said. "I am getting old and I tire of the constant fighting and this last attack by the Andromidans on our outpost has me worn thin but the Warlon people are not so easily changed. I will see what I can do as Emperor when the Warlon High Council convenes later this year. This is not a promise to join, I remind you."

"Understood, Emperor Clang," Gheron said. "I will give you all the time that you need to study the League documents that I have brought with me. I only hope you will have some good news for me when I return."

With that they grasped arms, said goodbye and Gheron headed back to Pogh.

It was almost a year to the day when the Andromidans attacked another Warlon outpost. Emperor Clang contacted Gheron and asked to meat with him. He immediately boarded the fastest ship in the Fleet. When Gheron arrived only six months later he immediately contacted Clang.

"What have you learned in regards to Joining with the League?" Gheron asked.

"As I had predicted, many Warlons were against it until the most recent attack by the Andromidans on our outpost on Getz several months ago" Clang said. "At that time there was a stranger that risked his own life to defend a Warlon. Come, follow me."

Clang led Gheron out of his office and down the hall to the Wall of Warriors and he told him that only those warriors that have shown great self-sacrifice, or those that have died honorably in battle for the Empire were listed on the wall. Gheron was looking at the wall and he spotted a fresh, new plaque among the older tarnished plaques. He stopped to look at it and he thought that he recognized the image portrayed there. Gheron read the inscription under the image and a cold shiver ran down his spine.

"This stranger, a human from Earth, had nearly gotten himself killed in battle while saving one of my Captains," Clang explained.

"This human who had fought alongside your Warlon fighters, is my son-in-law, Robert Larson." Gheron explained. "It doesn't surprise me that he would get involved. "There is no better way to learn about someone than to fight by his side." Robert told me that once. A very long time ago now."

When Clang heard this he realized that he now had the final piece of information he needed to convince the other members of the Warlon High Council that the time was right to stop the petty fighting between the Empire and the League and join them and sign the alliance. Gheron immediately called back to Pogh, contacted William and had him fly to Warlon. Standing together in the High Council chambers, the Warlon Emperor Clang signed the alliance officially ending their fighting and officially adding the Warlon race to The League of United Planets roster.

After the ceremony, Ambassador William asked Clang about Bob.

"He is an honored Warlon warrior now," Clang said. "He has proven to us that humans and Warlons are not so different after all. We are fierce in our loyalties and not afraid to jump into battle when the time comes. If the other races of the League are like the human Bob's, then I feel this alliance will prove worthwhile."

"How long did Bob stay on Warlon? When did he leave?" William asked.

"He was here for little more than a month," Clang said. "He left about nine months ago now. He said that he had to keep searching for his mate. I offered him one of my daughters but he declined."

"Did he say which way he was heading?" William asked.

"No he did not. Go and talk to Ktaal, he and Bob are brothers now," Clang said. "Maybe he knows."

"Thank you Emperor Clang," William said as he turned to find Ktaal.

William found Ktaal with his family; they were celebrating Ktaal's new Ambassador position.

"Excuse the interruption," William said. "I would like to speak with Ktaal about Bob..."

"That's Ambassador Ktaal to you," he said half drunk.

"Sorry, Ambassador Ktaal," William said. "My name is William Mont and I am the Ambassador from Vergon. Perhaps you have heard of me?

"Forgive me Ambassador," Ktaal said. "I forget my place sometimes. What can I do for you?

"I would like to talk to you about Bob, if you have some time," William said.

"He is my brother now," Ktaal said. "He has saved my life in battle."

"So I heard," William said. "Could you tell me about it?"

"I met him in a cantina on Cantoo," Ktaal said. "I was spoiling for a fight and when he walked into the cantina I headed right for him. I insulted him and tried to provoke him into a fight but he just told me that he was not interested in fighting. I told him that it was to bad because I was and then one thing led to another and we were fighting. But when the fight was over he had beaten my First Officer and me. I was impressed and admired his tenacity and we became friends."

"He followed us back to Warlon and when the Andromidans attacked Getz, he followed us there too. He helped us destroy three of their ships. But while we were on the surface an Andromidan dog tried to attack me from behind. Bob hollered and pushed me out of the way taking a pistol blast in the shoulder for his trouble. I killed the Andromidan dog where he stood. I turned my attention to Bob and asked him why he had saved me. He just said that he liked me. Crazy human. I picked him up and we transported up to my ship and I took him to the infirmary were he was stabilized as we flew back to Warlon. He recovered and was presented with the Warlon Medal of Honor, he stayed a few more weeks and then he had to leave. I owe him my life and, as I have said, we are now brothers and I would gladly give my life for him; I owe him that much."

"That is not the first time he has saved another's life," William said. "When I first met Bob on his home world of Earth he was also saving a mans life. I knew right then and there that I wanted to become his friend and I did. We became good friends and I miss what we had. So you can see that I am very interested in finding him. Did Bob tell you where he was going before he left?"

"No, he did not," Ktaal said. "He just said that he had to find his mate."

"Did you track his heading?" William asked "Yes we did," Ktaal said. "I will have the information sent to you immediately. I hope you find him well. I had only just gotten to know Bob for a short time and I can tell you this much, I have never met another being other then a Warlon that I would gladly give my life for until I had met him."

"Thank you Ktaal," William said. "I know the feeling."

The celebration on Warlon lasted a week, one thing you can say about the Warlons, they love an excuse to celebrate and drink.

William checked out the information that he received on the heading that Bob's ship, the Arrgott, had taken when he left Warlon almost one year earlier. He plotted the course on the star map; there were no less than a dozen worlds that he could visit if he continued on this course.

Many of them were undeveloped worlds and the Arrgott would know this so, unless she had to feed or there were some type of problem, she would avoid those. That left four potential planets on this course. When Ktaal was ready, they left for Pogh.

Lola was at the port to greet them when they arrived and when Gheron, William and Ktaal got to Pogh William excused himself and immediately boarded his personal ship and headed straight for Vergon. After William departed Lola turned to Gheron and asked him if William had ever done anything like this in the past.

"I wonder what that's all about? Just a hi and goodbye," Lola said as William headed off.

"I have known William for over two centuries now and I have never seen him go straight back to the Vergon home world after returning from a signing," He offered. "I saw him talking with ambassador Ktaal after the signing ceremony back on the Warlon home world, maybe he knows something. I will have a talk with him tomorrow after he has had a chance to settle in and find out if he knows why William left so quickly."

"Thank you Gheron," Lola said. "Keep me informed, I hope there isn't anything wrong."

"My pleasure Lola," Gheron said. "I will."

The following day Gheron spoke with Ktaal and he told him what he had discussed with William while on Warlon. Ktaal gave Gheron a copy of the sensor log that he had given to William. Gheron thanked Ktaal and took the sensor log back to his office where he sat down and studied it. Lola stopped by his office later that day and asked him if he had spoken with Ktaal. Gheron told Lola about the sensor log. She asked him if he knew what it meant.

"This is a copy of the sensor log that the Warlons made as the Arrgott left the planet and headed into space," Gheron said. "It tracks the ship out only a few days but I plotted the course and speed into the computer and it shows that the flight path would take him past several inhabited planets, none of which are League worlds yet. It would appear all but four are primitive or undeveloped worlds. William must know something and that is probably why he left for Vergon."

"Why didn't he tell you about it?" Lola asked.

"I don't know the answer to that question, Lola. But I do know that he must have his reasons," Gheron said. "And

I trust William enough to know that when he feels that the time is right he will let us know what those reasons are. We cannot press him on this. We must give him his time."

"I understand, you have known him for a very long time," Lola said. "I hope you are right."

"I know I am," Gheron stated.

"Okay then, thank you for your time Gheron," Lola said. And as she got up to leave she added, "Well I had better get back to work then. We'll talk some more."

Gheron and the rest of the council continued contacting new worlds and inviting them to join the League.

CHAPTER
THIRTEEN

When William landed on Vergon he contacted the Great Council and told them about the League's progress and how far it had come from its humbling beginnings as just an idea to where it was today. The Council was pleased and William was informed that he was to stay on Vergon. He asked for an explanation but was told that he would find out when the time was right.

William spent the time waiting by studying the sensor logs he received from Ktaal. He followed the progress of the League by reading every report that came in from the League Council. He was in contact with Gheron personally by hyperspace radio as well. Almost a year had passed and finally William was called in front of the great council.

"Mr. Mont, we appreciate your waiting," Chancellor Torrell, the Great Council leader, said. "Please sit. How have you been?"

"I am well," he answered. "Thank you for asking." "Good, I am glad to hear that," Torrell said. "One of the reasons why we have asked you here today is that we have some questions to ask."

"OK," William replied. "What is it that you would like to know?"

"Right. How would you describe your relationship with the Earth human, Robert Larson?" He asked.

"Well. Robert and I had become good friends shortly after I had met him for the first time on Earth nearly three hundred years ago," He answered. "There had been a terrible accident and Robert was literally holding a mans life in his hands..."

"We are aware of the incident," Torrell interrupted. "We have read your report about it."

"Okay," William said. "Is there something wrong that I should know about?"

"No," Torrell replied. "We just want to know more of your thoughts about him, that's all. Like, how you feel about him traveling through space making contact with other races. And perhaps how it is that this primitive human could make you become his friend. That's all."

"First of all," William started. "Bob did not "make" me become his friend. After I had seen what he had done when I first met him on Earth back then, and after talking with him, I had this feeling that this man was destined for something greater then him. I knew then that I wanted to be his friend and I wanted him to be my friend as well.

And as to him traveling through space. Who are we to say what one man can or can not do? You all know as well as I that we cannot interfere with the course of these things. That we must let them play out the way that they are intended to. I was proud to watch over him while I was stationed on Earth and I was careful not to influence him in anything that he had done. I would do the same today. The fact that he is still alive today speaks volumes about his will and spirit."

"We understand that William," Torrell said. "We get the same feeling about this human as well and most of us here have never met the man. In all our millennia as a species there have only been a few beings that have ever caused such a disturbance. We were only hoping you could shed some light on this one; that's all."

"Disturbance? What? Do you think that Bob is bad?" William asked.

"No, no. That's not what I meant at all," Torrell said. "What we are feeling is a good thing; you already know that. You just said so yourself that you felt it in him. We are merely trying to understand him a little better that is all. For instance, how was it that of all the places you could have chosen to stay on Earth, you chose the same area as Mr. Larson? How was it that of all the places that Gheron's scout ship could have crashed, it crashed on Mr. Larson's property? You see the questions? We were just hoping that you could give us some insight about him."

"I apologize Chancellor," William said. "I can't explain why I chose to settle there to do my observations anymore than the others can explain why they chose much larger, more populated regions to observe. I took a look at the sensor data that we had of Earth and that area just seemed right. It was as if I were drawn to the region. As for Gheron's scout ship; well, Earth is a big planet and the fact that it came down in my area and on Bob's farm, I don't know that either. A higher force had to have had a hand in it. Bringing us together. Showing us this human. There has to be a good reason. One we are not fully aware of yet. And the fact that so many races and worlds have become members of the League of United Planets after having been contacted by this strange human from a distant world that they knew nothing about; shows me that Bob's true character is genuine, it cannot be faked. These races, highly intelligent races, were truly inspired by this man and if he were faking his true nature I am sure that it would have been discovered. These races had nothing but praise for Bob when we talked with them."

"We know this," Torrell replied. "Everyone here has read the reports and we have been keeping up with current events. There was some concern by some of the members of the council that you had gotten to close to the human Bob to think clearly that is all. I just want to be sure that is not the case."

"I assure you sir, and the members of the Council that I have never been more clear in my thinking," William replied. "If I thought that my judgment were clouded, in any way, I would step down as Ambassador immediately."

"There will be no need for that William," Torrell stated. "Your actions over the past several hundred years prove that. The Great Elders want you to continue watching over this human they feel he has earned that. So, we have a new ship for you. One of seven new prototypes and it is fully loaded and ready to depart when you are.

The other six ships will follow you to Pogh where they will be tested and eventually added to the fleet. Thank you for all that you have done so far and good luck."

"Thank you sir," William replied. "But I'm afraid that I do not know where Bob is at this time. It seems that he has traveled off into deep space after leaving Warlon. I have plotted his course but there is no way to know if he has stayed on it. I am afraid that I have lost touch with him for now. Gheron and I both have come close but it would appear that we are always just a few steps behind him. We will continue searching for him though; no matter how long it takes."

"I have no doubt that you will see him some day," Torrell said. "Do not give up hope."

"Thank you sir I will not," William said. "If you have nothing else then I will be heading back to Pogh in the morning. Good day sir."

"That is all. Good luck," Torrell said as William left the Council chambers.

William was eager to get back to Pogh and as soon as he had packed up a few belongings he was taken to the spaceport where he boarded a shuttle and was taken to the orbiting ships. He saw his new ship, it was huge, the Captain welcomed him on board and as soon as he was settled in they headed for Pogh.

The trip to Pogh only took about six months; the new prototype ships were faster then any ship currently in Space fleet. News of Williams's arrival back from Vergon with the new ships didn't take long to reach Gheron and he and Burgess, the Admiral of Space Fleet, were eager to see the new ships. These new engine designs were capable of maintaining light speed nine while topping out at eleven for short durations. The prototypes had triple redundant primary shields with secondary shielding as well. The weapons were also new; full three hundred and sixty degree plasma beams and anti-matter torpedoes.

They had multiple cold fusion reactors for auxiliary power generation should their main engines go off-line. When fully stocked, the crew of six hundred could stay out for six years. When they passed the fleet trails and were accepted; Space Fleet put in an order for fifty more ships. They would become a valuable addition to the Space Fleet line. A few months later, after things settled back down, Gheron called on William to talk.

"Hello William," Gheron said as he entered his office. "Are you busy?"

"Never to busy for you my friend," William replied. "What can I do for you?"

"I know you did not go back to Vergon to pick up some new ships," Gheron said. "Can you tell me what is going on?"

"Yes, sorry about that. I had received a message from Vergon on the way back from Warlon," William said. "The Council wanted to see me. Eventually they asked me more questions about Bob. I told them all that I knew. It seemed that he had caught the attention of the Great Elders…"

"Is that bad?" Gheron asked.

"That was my question," William replied. "The answer was no. It seems they want me to keep an eye on him…"

"We do not know where he is!" Gheron stated.

"I told the Council Chancellor that very same thing," William continued. "I was told to do the best that I could."

"What can we do?" Gheron asked.

"I want to send one of the new ships out on the same course that Bob took when he left Warlon," William replied. "He's got about a five-year head start by now, but I have no other ideas."

"That sounds like a good plan William," Gheron said. "Who did you have in mind for Captain? I've heard great things about a Commander Oran from Thoria. He graduated top in his class at the academy. Rose to rank of Commander in half the time it normally takes. He is currently serving on the Delco, Captained by George Franco. He has just recommended him for his own command."

"You read my mind Gheron," William said. "Let us go see what Admiral Burgess thinks."

The two men left to talk to the Admiral and after only a few minutes he agreed.

"I like the mission," Burgess said. "And if both of you think that Commander Oran is your man then who am I to argue?"

"You are the Admiral of Space Fleet," Gheron said. "It is up to you to decide."

"Right!" Burgess said. "But if two of the top Ambassadors from the League Council come to me with a recommendation, I'm sure as hell not about to refuse."

"We are not trying to influence your decision," William said. "It is just that we have heard good things about him."

"As have I," Burgess said. "I was looking to find a command for him anyway. It seems this mission has come at an opportune time. I will contact Captain Franco and have him return. He should be here in a few days."

"Thank you Admiral Burgess," Gheron said. "Don't thank me yet," Burgess said. "Why?" Gheron asked.

"Because you and Ambassador William get to sit down and explain this mission to him," Burgess replied. "I'm giving him to you. From now on he takes his orders from you two."

"Understood," William said. "Thank you again Admiral. We will be waiting for him."

When the Delco arrived Captain Franco and Commander Oran beamed down and headed for the admirals office.

"Why does the Admiral want to see us?" Commander Oran asked as they readied themselves for beam down.

"I don't know. He probably heard about that stunt you pulled on Star Base two ten," Captain Franco offered.

When they reached the Admiral's office, Burgess gave Commander Oran his new orders. Captain Franco had his pick of a new first officer. Commander Oran headed off to meet with Ambassadors William Mont and Gheron. "Come right in Commander…I mean Captain Oran,"

Gheron said when he arrived. "Please have a seat." "Aye sir," Oran said as he sat down.

"Have you had a chance to study your new orders?" William asked.

"Briefly sir," Oran replied. "Is this a rescue mission?" "No," William replied. "We will explain what we need."

For the next few hours William explained what it was he needed Oran to do. Oran agreed to take on the mission.

"I know it is a long shot," William said. "But it is the only shot I know. The ship you will be commanding is the Pegasus. It is one of the newest. It was designed to be out for six years with a full compliment, but it has been reconfigured for this mission and you will be running with a third less crew so you should be able to add another four to five years onto that. Once you reach our outpost on Warlon and are topped off you will be on your own.

Contact the worlds along the projected flight path and be careful. If you get new information follow through as best you can and report it to us immediately. If you have not found out anything definite or have not made contact in five years return to the nearest star base and we will go from there."

"Understood Ambassador," Oran said.

"Good luck Captain Oran, and God speed," William offered.

"Thank you Ambassador," Oran said as he saluted and then went to take command of his new ship.

CHAPTER
FOURTEEN

Three years after the new ships came on line Lola was leading three of them out to Zephyr. She was enjoying the fact that the faster engines cut the travel time by half. As the convoy approached Andromidan space Lola called the Captains of the other ships to tell them not to get any closer then five hundred thousand kilometers to the boarder. Lola ordered all ships to maintain maximum sensor range and to be on alert for any signs of the Andromidans.

The little convoy was about a week out from Zephyr territory when their long-range sensors picked up a disturbance. Lola ordered the ships to stop, raise shields and then ordered the Captains of the ships to set their weapons to half power and fire their plasma beams in all directions. As soon as the weapons fired an Andromidan ship flickered into view a few thousand kilometers to their port. Detected, the Andromidan ship fired its weapons on the lead ship and then disappeared once again. The improved shields held fast. The Captain of the lead ship contacted the Andromidan ship and told the Commander to leave League space. It fired once again onto the convoy so the Captain ordered the tactical officer to target three new anti-matter torpedoes, full spread, at the Andromidan ships location and fire. One of the torpedoes found its mark and the Andromidan ship burst into flames and was destroyed.

Suddenly five more Andromidan war ships appeared and surrounded the small convoy and the Commander of the lead ship, Commander Pell, demanded their immediate surrender. Lola informed Commander Pell that her ships were violating Zephyr free space and if they did not leave at once she would have them destroyed.

Infuriated, she ordered her ships to destroy the League convoy. The Andromidans opened fire but the improved shields held fast and the convoy suffered no damage. Lola once again contacted Commander Pell and quite bluntly ordered her to stand down or be destroyed.

The Andromidan ships moved off a few thousand kilometers and then turned to fire another volley. Lola, annoyed by this act, ordered her ships to target all weapons full power on the attacking vessels and fire when ready. The Andromidan ships fired once again with little results and then the three League ships unleashed the full power of their new ships weaponry destroying all five of the enemy vessels. When the smoke of battle cleared, Lola regrouped her convoy and resumed her course to Zephyr. She sent a report back to Space Fleet and the League Council detailing the assault once she reached Zephyr.

Space Fleet Admiral Burgess contacted Emperor Turrzok of Andromidan to inform him that if his ships did not stop violating the borders between their two factions then they would have no choice but to impose sanctions on them.

"Your United League Space Fleet has no authority over us," Emperor Turrzok stated. "We are within our rights to expand our Empire as you have expanded yours."

"The League does not mind that you expand your Empire," Admiral Burgess replied. "It is how you are going about expanding your Empire that concerns us. You are attacking systems and taking by force what you want and we will not stand idly by as you do so."

"Your ships just attacked and destroyed six Andromidan science vessels," Turrzok stated. "They were unarmed and mapping the boarder."

"Don't try and hand me that shit Turrzok. Your ships were over five hundred thousand kilometers on the wrong side of the boarder and you know it. And when they were caught, your "unarmed" science vessels attacked our ships," Admiral Burgess explained. "Our ships were merely defending themselves."

"Your ships fired first," Turrzok barked.

"Only low level plasma beams, in order to expose your ships," Burgess replied. "And when one was discovered the Commander was told to leave. She did not. Instead she chose to fire on our ships and it cost her her ship and crew. And then five more of your so-called "science" vessels decided to ambush our ships ending with the same results. Hear me now Turrzok, any more unauthorized incursions into League space by any of your ships will be treated like an act of war and will be dealt with severely."

"That sounds very much like a declaration of war Admiral," Turrzok stated. "If it is war you want, war you will get."

"Take it however you will Emperor," Burgess replied. "You have been warned. We will not stand for any more attacks." And with that the Admiral closed the channel.

For the next several years the League prepared for the worst by bolstering the defenses of all the outer League systems. They set up larger; more fully equipped Star Bases on many more planets between the more distant League worlds. Now the League Space Fleet could come to the aid of most all of the unified systems within days instead of months.

During much of that time the League of United Planets experienced peaceful coexistence throughout the quadrant. It seemed that the Andromidans were not interested in starting any real wars. Newer, larger and more powerful ships were being built. These ships could travel at light speed twelve and carry crews of over one thousand. Many new science and exploration vessels were built as well; their missions were to map and search the quadrant for alien worlds that were coming of age. They would make contact with any planet that had settled into peaceful existence and developed light speed capabilities and offer their support and the opportunity to join the League if they wanted to.

One day Space Fleet received a report that an outpost that had been set up in a distant part of the quadrant had been attacked and was completely destroyed. Space Fleet sent two of their ships to investigate and when they arrived they found the outpost gutted, smoldering and all of the inhabitants either dead or missing. As they were finishing their investigation their sensors picked up a large ship approaching at an incredibly high speed. Suddenly they were facing a ship that dwarfed their own. Their records indicated that it was very much like the Cyborg ship that attacked and nearly totally destroyed the Berillion home world over two hundred and twenty years earlier.

A message was sent back to Space Fleet and when it arrived a message was sent back to get the hell out of there.

The ships quickly turned and as they headed back towards the nearest Star Base they were overtaken by the Cyborg ship and attacked. They returned fire and knocked out the pursuing ships engines. They continued at top speed and sent their report back to Space Fleet. They had only traveled a few more hours when their sensors picked up the Cyborg ship closing fast. When the ship reached them it fired its weapons and effortlessly destroyed the two Space Fleet ships and then continued on to the Star Base where it wiped out the inhabitants there as well.

The Cyborgs then continued on to the next Star Base but when it arrived the Space Fleet was waiting for them with over fifty of their newest battle ships. The battle was long and difficult and lasted for two days. The Cyborgs were finally defeated but not without great loss to the Space Fleet armada. Nearly half the ships were either destroyed or disabled; it was a costly battle but it also provided Space Fleet with the valuable information it needed to be able to quickly defeat these Cyborg creatures should they try and attack again anytime soon.

CHAPTER
FIFTEEN

It took a few years for Space Fleet and the League to recover after the incident with the Cyborgs. And during that time the League Council ordered Space Fleet to position sensor beacons around the perimeter of the known League space. These beacons would serve as an early warning system and would be able to give the League enough warning should the Cyborgs return. On one such mission to deploy these beacons the Space Fleet exploration vessel, the U.S.S. Patton/C, Captained by Ron Hurt, had just deployed the fourth of her five beacons when the ships sensors started blaring.

"Report!" Captain Hurt demanded.

"Long range sensors are picking up a strange disturbance dead ahead sir," Lt. Callum the tactical officer replied. "Distance, ten million kilometers."

"Shields up! Red alert," the first officer, Commander Fellows ordered.

"All stop!" The Captain ordered. "Open all hailing channels."

"Hailing channels open sir," communications officer Lt. Tibor replied.

"This is Captain Hurt of The League of United Planets vessel the U.S.S. Patton," Hurt started. "Whatever or whoever is out there, you are on a collision course with our vessel. Please alter your course and respond if you can hear this."

There was no response as the unknown disturbance continued on its current course.

"Helm, steer twenty degrees starboard and start ahead at one quarter light speed," Captain Hurt ordered.

The helmsman, Ensign Burke, input the commands and the ship moved out of the path of the oncoming vessel.

"Sir, sensors now show that the unknown disturbance has altered course and is still heading straight for us," the tactical officer reported.

"Contact Space Fleet and advise them of the situation," Captain Hurt ordered. "Full magnification on forward screen."

They could see nothing at first and then Commander Fellows, pointed to a part of the screen and said, "There, it looks like some sort of distortion among the stars."

"Very good Commander," the Captain stated. "I want a full sensor sweep of that area with everything we got."

"Sensors are picking up and exhaust trail and the infrared confirms there's a heat signature," Lt. Callum reported. "It certainly appears to be a ship and it doesn't appear to be in any hurry either. It is currently traveling at forty percent of light speed Captain."

"Arm weapons," Commander Fellows stated.

"Belay that order," Captain Hurt ordered. "Steer thirty degrees port and increase our speed to fifty percent light speed."

"Captain!" Commander Fellows started. "We should at least arm our weapons for our own safety."

"Understood Commander. But I don't want to send the wrong message should the ships crew be friendly." the Captain stated.

"Sir sensors indicate the alien ship has altered its course again and has increased its speed to match our own. It's still on an intercept course with the Patton," Lt. Callum reported. "Distance out is now five million kilometers and slowly closing sir."

"All stop," the Captain ordered. "It's apparent that the Captain of that ship isn't about to give up so we might as well sit here and wait for it. Keep shields at maximum but make no move that could be interpreted as hostile."

"I don't like it," Commander Fellows stated. "We should just go to maximum light speed and get the hell out of here."

"Part of our mission is to meet new races," Captain Hurt stated. "We wouldn't be doing our jobs if every time we came across a race we didn't know or understand we just ran away or worse fired our weapons at them. We wouldn't get anything done."

Suddenly a strange red beam appeared, fanned out and engulfed the Patton.

"Sir, it appears we are being scanned," Lt. Callum reported.

"Let's try hailing the ship again. Use full spectrum Universal Translator," Captain Hurt said. "Maybe they will answer us now."

"Hailing frequencies open sir," Lt. Tibor reported. "This is Captain Hurt of the League of United Planets vessel the U.S.S. Patton," Hurt stated. "We are on a peaceful exploration mission and we would like to talk and learn more about you, please respond."

"Still no response Captain," Lt. Tibor reported.

Suddenly the Patton's proximity alarm started blaring and the alien ship became visible on the screen. It totally dwarfed the Patton and it was still over one hundred thousand kilometers away. It made no attempt to alter its course, speed or to communicate with the Patton.

"Evasive maneuvers," Commander Fellows ordered. "Full up on the bow thrusters and ahead half light speed now."

The Patton pitched up and shot out of the path of the oncoming ship narrowly avoiding the collision. The alien vessel kept on its course never once slowing or making any attempt to communicate or acknowledging the Patton's presence. And when it was twenty thousand kilometers away, it vanished again.

"That was close," Commander Fellows remarked. "To close," Captain Hurt replied.

"Should we follow them?" Commander Fellows asked. "No," Captain Hurt replied. "We'll send the report and logs to Space Fleet and let them handle it. We have a mission to continue with. Set course to the next set of coordinates Ensign Burke, light speed six."

"Aye sir," Ensign Burke replied as he manipulated the helm controls. "Course plotted, laid in and speed set Captain."

"Initiate," the Captain said.

Ensign Burke manipulated the controls and the ship jumped to light speed and away from the area. The Patton reached the new coordinates two days later and the crew launched the last of her beacons without incident. Captain Ron Hurt contacted Space Fleet from his staff room and informed them that they had completed the task. Space Fleet Command asked him if they had any more encounters with the strange alien craft and he reported back that they did not. Then Space Fleet informed Captain Hurt that they had another mission for him and they sent him the file. Space Fleet told him that the mission was vital and could be one of the most important ones since the alliance with the Warlons.

After the call from Space Fleet, Captain Hurt called his senior officers into the staff room for the briefing. "We've been given a new mission," Captain Hurt started. "After a brief stop over on Star Base two zero seven for supplies and to change out a few crew members whose enlistment is up, we will be heading out into deep space. Space Fleet has detected an alien signal and when it was translated it was determined to be an open invitation for contact.

I've been informed that it will take Space fleet a few weeks to get a fully equipped Star ship ready to head to that area. Since we are the closest ship in the area we are ordered to respond. It will take us a little over six months at top speed to reach the coordinates where the signal originated from and we do not know what we will find when we get there.

This will be a good chance to prove to the rest of he galaxy that the League of United Planets is passionate about their mission statement. I only hope that we can represent the League well. Are there any questions or concerns?"

Commander Fellows spoke first and said, "I believe I speak for the entire crew when I tell you that we are behind you and this mission one hundred percent. You can count on us to do our best to make this a success."

The remainder of the staff officers nodded in agreement and with that the Captain dismissed them and they headed to Star Base two zero seven and after a few days they were resupplied and with the new crew members quartered they headed out into the unknown. The Captain sent back weekly reports as they sped towards the unknown system. All of the science teams were busy gathering information as they went along. Star charts had to be adjusted or new ones had to be made as they made their way through the new unexplored region of space.

CHAPTER
SIXTEEN

Admiral Anderson of Space Fleet called Captain Jonathan W. Pierce, the Captain of the newest League flagship the U.S.S. Duncan D, into his office.

"Sit down Captain," Admiral Anderson said as Captain Pierce entered his office.

"Thank you Admiral," Pierce said as he sat down. "What can I do for you?"

"We've picked up a transmission from an alien race out in an uncharted region of space," Admiral Anderson started. "I understand your ship has just returned from its shake down cruise. I read your report so I know it's ready. Since your ship is the only one available we need you to go out, rendezvous with the Patton and make contact. The trip should take you about five or six months. Right now we have the Patton on route, they should get there about two weeks before you but they are equipped to do little more then investigate and assess the situation. Here is the file and all the information you will need for this mission. You will leave in five days, have your ship and crew ready."

"Understood Admiral," Captain Pierce replied. "We will be ready."

"Good," the Admiral said. "Do you have any concerns with the ship or crew?"

"No sir," Captain Pierce replied. "The ship is fantastic and I have full confidence in my crew. We are ready for this mission."

"Thank you Jonathan," the Admiral said. "You are excused, good luck and God speed."

"Thank you Admiral," Captain Pierce replied as he rose and left the office.

The Duncan was made ready and when it was time to depart the Captain ordered Lieutenant Droid to set course to the coordinates given them in the file.

"Open a channel to the Station Harbor Master Lt. Braag," the Captain ordered.

"Channel open sir," Lt. Braag replied.

"This is Captain Jonathan Pierce of the Duncan," Pierce stated. "Request permission to disembark."

"Permission to disembark granted," came the voice of the Harbor Master from the speakers.

At that point the docking clamps disengaged and the umbilicals retracted.

"Lt. Commander Droid," Captain Pierce ordered. "Take us out.

Thrusters only."

"Aye sir," Lt. Droid replied as he manipulated the helm controls.

The Duncan's maneuvering thrusters fired and the big new star ship slowly moved away from the dock; when it was clear of all moorings Lt. Commander Droid fired up the sub-light engines and they moved away at one-one hundredth of light speed. When the Duncan cleared the space station Droid fired up the Light speed engines and the Duncan sped away at light speed eight. Two weeks into the journey the Duncan neared Star Base one five one and they stopped briefly to pick up the League Ambassador Gaylon and her aid and then they continued on their way.

CHAPTER SEVENTEEN

Meanwhile, the U S S Patton neared the coordinates and they dropped out of light speed and slowed to half-light. They entered a binary system with twelve planets.

"I wonder where the welcoming committee is?" Commander Fellows asked.

"Set scanners to maximum," Captain Hurt ordered. "Let's see if anyone's home."

"Sensors are showing two class-M planets," Lt. Callum reported. Fourth and fifth planets out from the suns."

"Life signs?" Captain Hurst asked.

"We're too far out to get any clear readings," Lt. Callum reported as he manipulated some controls on his console. "I'm experiencing interference from the solar radiation."

"Any danger to the ship or crew?" Captain Hurt asked. "No sir," Lt. Callum replied. "We're in no danger." "Take us in," Captain Hurt ordered. "One-quarter light."

"Aye sir," Ensign Burke replied. "One-quarter light." "I don't like this," Commander Fellows said. "It's too damn quiet. We are at the proper coordinates, right?" "Yes Commander,"

Ensign Burke replied. "These are the coordinates given by Space Fleet."

"We should be getting signs of civilization," Commander Fellows said. "Any radio chatter?"

"Nothing on any known channels," Lt. Tibor replied. "I'm scanning all frequencies now."

Lt. Tibor scanned through the frequencies for several minutes.

"Sir, I'm picking up some sort of automated signal," Lt. Tibor reported. "Very low band and very low frequency. It appears to be coming from the outer-most planet. By my calculations the signal strength it would have taken over twenty-five years before it was detected. Who detected the signal?"

"Admiral Anderson said that the Vergons had detected the signal and decoded it," Captain Hurt explained. "It was sent to Space Fleet for follow up investigation."

"Do we check out the signal first or the class-M planets Captain?" Commander Fellows asked.

"Ensign Burke, set new course to the source of the signal and put us into standard orbit," Captain Hurt ordered.

"Aye sir," Ensign Burke replied as he manipulated the controls.

It took the Patton a few minutes to reach the planet and establish an orbit over the source of the signal.

"Report Lt. Callum," the Captain ordered.

"Sensors show no atmosphere or life-signs Captain," Lt. Callum reported. "I'm detecting a large structure. The signal is emanating from there."

"Conditions Lieutenant?" The Captain asked. "Twilight at best on the day side of the planet, minus one hundred and eighty degrees Celsius, no wind so that's good and nominal radiation," Lt. Callum reported.

"Form your away team, Commander. Arctic protocol," Captain Hurt ordered. "Take a shuttle craft and stay in constant communication."

"Aye sir. Callum you're with me," Commander Fellows said as he left the bridge.

Commander Fellows and Lt. Callum prepped the shuttle and after donning sub-arctic space suits they were ready to depart. Commander Fellows had just ordered the shuttle bay doors open when he received a message from the Captain.

"Commander Fellows," the Captain said. "Fellows here, go ahead Captain," he replied.

"Change of plans. The signal just stopped and is now emanating from the fifth planet," Hurt stated. "Return to the bridge while we relocate."

"Understood," Fellows answered.

Commander Fellows and Lt. Callum reached the bridge and took their stations just as the Patton established orbit over the fifth planet.

"Sensors detect a large metropolis with the signal coming from a central location," Lt. Callum reported. "No life-signs detected, radiation within norms, moderate temperatures and the atmosphere is compatible."

"Thank you Lt.," Captain Hurt replied. "What now?" Commander Fellows asked.

"You and Lt. Callum report to shuttle bay one and stand by," the Captain ordered. "Shuttle bay one, prepare a shuttle for remote flight and open doors on my command."

"Shuttle ready," came the voice over the speaker. "Open doors now," Captain Hurt ordered.

The shuttle bay doors opened and the Captain stepped over to helm control.

"I'll take over from here Ensign," the Captain said as he sat down at the console.

Captain Hurt manipulated the controls and the empty shuttle lifted up off the deck and exited the ship. Captain Hurt piloted the shuttle to the city and landed it next to the structure and the signal continued. After waiting several minutes he piloted the shuttle back to the ship and into the bay.

"Commander Fellows," Captain Hurt said. "Take her down."

"On our way," Commander Fellows replied.

Commander Fellows and Lt. Callum re-entered the shuttle and just as they were about to proceed out the door, the Captain called them and told them that the signal had stopped again. Commander Fellows and Lt. Callum returned to the bridge.

"It seems that we are being tested," Commander Fellows said as he entered the bridge.

"You may be right Commander," Captain Hurt said. "The signal is now coming from the fourth planet," Lt.

Tibor reported.

"Thank you Lt.," Hurt replied. "Open hailing frequencies, all channels and all frequencies."

"Open Captain," Lt. Tibor replied.

"This is Captain Hurt of the U.S.S. Patton, from the League of United Planets," he started. "We are here and awaiting contact. Please respond."

"No response sir and the signal from the fourth planet just intensified," Lt. Tibor reported.

"What are we going to do next?" Commander Fellows asked.

THE LEAGUE OF UNITED PLANETS

"I want you to take a shuttle down to this planet, don't exit, keep your shields up and stand by," Captain Hurt stated. "Lt. Callum, you take another shuttle to the fourth planet, establish orbit, locate the source of the signal and stand by. I'll take the Patton to the outer planet and then we'll see what happens. Go."

Once the two shuttles were in position they contacted the Patton.

"Shuttle one in position," Commander Fellows reported.

"Shuttle two in position," Lt. Callum reported as well.

"Acknowledged," Captain Hurt stated. "Lt. Tibor, what's the status of the signal?"

"Still coming from the fourth planet sir," Lt. Tibor replied.

"Understood," Captain Hurt replied. "Lt. Callum, take the shuttle down please."

"Aye sir," Lt. Callum replied as he broke orbit and proceeded to land at the site of the signal.

When Lt. Callum's shuttle was less then one hundred kilometers from the source of the signal, it stopped.

"Sir…" Lt. Tibor started.

"Don't tell me," Captain Hurt stated. "The signal stopped!"

"Yes sir," Lt. Tibor replied. "How did you…?" "We're definitely being tested!" Captain Hurt stated.

"Where is the signal coming from now?"

"The signal has stopped transmitting completely sir," Lt. Tibor replied.

"Helm, reestablish orbit over the fifth planet," Captain Hurt ordered. "Patton to Commander Fellows. Please return to the ship. Lt. Callum. Please return to the Patton."

"Acknowledged," Lt. Callum replied.

"Lt. Tibor," Hurt said. "Contact the Duncan and apprise them of our situation. Perhaps they can speed up their arrival time."

"Aye sir," Lt. Tibor replied as she manipulated the com. controls. "Sir. Captain Pierce of the Duncan reports that they should be able to rendezvous with us in seven days."

"Very good," Hurt said. "Let's see what we can learn in a week."

Once the shuttles were secured, the Captain called for a staff meeting in his ready room.

"Well Commander," Hurt started. "It would appear you were right. I think this is some sort of test to determine our intentions. Any suggestions?"

"How about sending a team down to the planet in a shuttle," Fellows started. "They can start a search at the site of the signal and record all their findings while we take up orbit over the fourth planet and send a team down to do a search there."

"Do you think it's wise to leave the search team alone while we are not in a position to offer support?" Lt. Callum asked.

"What better way to prove that we are willing to trust whoever is sending the signal," Hurt replied. "Maybe this is part of the test. I'm willing to believe that if we show that we are willing to expose ourselves, so to speak, then maybe we can gain the trust of the people that sent the message in return."

"I agree Captain," Commander Fellows replied. "What about the structure on the ice planet?" Lt. Tibor asked. "That's where the signal was coming from when we first arrived in this system."

"Maybe it is a decoy," Lt. Callum offered. "A way to test whoever responds to the signal. That way, if the planet gets attacked then nobody gets hurt and there is no signal from the inner planets."

"And since we didn't attack and only sent a shuttle," Fellows added. "Whoever is controlling the signal determined that we weren't a threat. And they activated the signal on the inner planet."

"That's possible," Lt. Tibor said. "But I don't think we should ignore the outer planet altogether. That still might be part of the test. How far are we willing to go to make contact?"

"Agreed," Hurt stated. "Commander Fellows, gather your away team and take a shuttle down to the surface. Lt. Callum will take a shuttle and his team will land on the other planet. When you are clear we will go to the ice planet and start our search there. Dismissed."

With that they started their investigation. Lt. Callum and his team were exploring the city on the fourth planet. They had spent twenty-four hours inside the structure where the signal had been sent from and were unable to detect any power source. He plotted a grid pattern and had his team search slowly and carefully each area. They were on their fourth day when one of the team members located a library and contacted the Lieutenant. The team spent the next twenty-four hours recording information.

Meanwhile, down on the fifth planet commander Fellows and his team were searching a similar pattern when they discovered an underground spaceport of some kind on their fifth day of investigation. There were two ships still sitting on the tarmac. They were large and commander Fellows guessed that they were transport ships used for interplanetary travel.

Commander Fellows approached the side of one of the ships and scanned it as he slowly made his way around it. He noticed that they had the same name but that they were numbered differently. One of his Lieutenants, Lt. Jones an archaeologist, said that they appeared to be shuttle craft. from a much larger ship.

"If these are shuttle craft.," Fellows said. "Then the ship they came from must be enormous."

"By my calculations," Lt. Jones said. "The mother ship would be over four times the size of the Patton. I suggest we proceed with extreme caution."

"Understood," Commander Fellows said.

When Commander Fellows walked around to the front of the shuttle craft. the interior lights came on and a panel opened and a ramp slid out. Then the other shuttles interior lights came on but it didn't open up. He immediately contacted the Captain who told him to wait until he could get back to them.

Captain Hurt recalled his away teams but they had lost contact with two of the team members. He contacted Fellows and told him that there would be a slight delay and then he said that he should proceed with caution when examining the alien shuttles. Hurt then sent down a three- man search party to the away teams last known position and started calling on the radio. Their search was hampered by the weather, which had turned from bad to worse. With an average mean temperature of minus one hundred and eighty degrees Celsius the working conditions were tenuous at best. It was full on darkness and the temperature was dropping fast. Their space suits would protect them from the cold but they were also bulky and they doubled their workload.

The search party followed the tracks of the missing away team members into a room that appeared to have been used as a lab. The tracks ended in the center of the room. There were only the tracks going in and nothing going back out. Scans of the room indicated that there was some sort of power source active. As the search team approached the center of the room a white light activated and shown down on a two-meter circle in the center of the room. They reported back to the Patton and Hurt told them to stand by. Hurt ordered a small probe be beamed down to the search party and they were instructed to set it in the center of the circle and see what happened.

The probe was maneuvered into the center of the circle but nothing happened. One of the techs stepped in to retrieve it and with a flash of light he disappeared. Lt.

Commander Thomas, the away team leader and chief engineer, called Captain Hurt immediately to inform him of the situation. Captain Hurt was starting to get annoyed. Unable to establish a link to the probe or the now three missing crew members; he gave the bridge to Lt. Tibor and prepared to beam down to the surface himself.

Captain Hurt joined the search team and after attempting to reestablish contact and failing, he said that he was going in.

"Captain," Lt. Commander Thomas said. "We can't afford to lose you as well. I'll go in. If we're not able to get back to this room by the time the Duncan arrives you should cut your losses and leave."

"I'll not leave anyone behind," Captain Hurt stated. "I'm not about to put anyone else at risk. My duty is to the ship and the safety of the crew."

"In that case I'm going with you," Lt. Commander Thomas said as he drew his weapon from its holster.

"Hold it!" Hurt stated. "Were the missing crew members armed?"

"Yes. We all are," Lt. Commander Thomas replied. "Why?"

"I have an idea," Captain Hurt stated. "We're going to leave our weapons here. I have a feeling we are still being tested."

"I don't like the idea of going in unarmed," Lt. Commander Thomas said.

"Neither do I," Captain Hurt said. "But I have a feeling it's all about trust. We'll leave our weapons on that table over there and that's an order."

Reluctantly Lt. Commander Thomas and the other crewman placed their weapons on the table with Captain Hurt's and then the three of them stepped into the circle and disappeared. Instantly the Captain and his team found themselves standing in a room identical to the one that they had just left. At first He thought that nothing had happened until he glanced over to the table and noticed their weapons were missing. Suddenly lights came on inside the room. Lt. Commander Thomas scanned the room with the scanner and reported his findings to the Captain.

"Sir," he started. "Scans indicate the temperature is rising and a breathable atmosphere is being maintained. Scans are also indicating a build up in power and it appears that some sort of energy field has been created around the building we are in."

The speaker crackled in Captain Hurt's helmet. "Patton to Captain Hurt. Come in please," Lt. Tibor's voice said.

"Hurt here," he replied. "What is it?"

"Sir," Lt. Tibor said. "We are detecting a power surge emanating from the structure you're in."

"Thank you Lt.," Hurt said. "We are well aware of it. "Can you scan us?"

"Yes sir we can," Lt. Tibor replied.

"Any life signs other then ours?" the Captain asked. "Yes. Three others," Tibor replied. "They appear to be our missing crew members."

"Where are they?" the captain asked.

"There's another room," Tibor replied. "Ten meters down the corridor outside the room you're in."

"Right or left of us?" Hurt asked.

"That would be your left Captain," Lt. Tibor offered. "Thank you Lt.," Hurt said. "Keep an eye on us. Hurt out."

"Aye sir," Tibor replied.

The Captain moved to the door and it opened. He stepped out into the corridor and paused. He reached up to remove his helmet and Lt. Commander Thomas stopped him.

"Sir," he said. "What are you doing?"

"Trust Commander Thomas," was all Hurt said as he removed his helmet and took a breath. "The air is fine."

The rest of the party removed their helmets as well. "This is Captain Hurt to Lt. Smith," Hurt called on the radio. "Do you copy?"

"Smith here," he replied. "Yes I can sir. Where are you sir? What's happening? We're reading an energy build up."

"We're ten meters away," Hurt replied. "It would seem that our hosts are welcoming us. Step out into the corridor please."

"We tried to sir," Smith stated. "The door is locked and we can't get out."

"Remain calm," Hurt said. "We'll come to you. We'll be there in a second."

"Aye sir," Smith replied.

Hurt and his team walked the few meters down the corridor to the door. He stepped in front of it and slowly walked towards it but nothing happened. Lt. Commander Thomas scanned the door for an external latch but found nothing.

"Sir," he said. "My scans indicate that the room is still void of life support."

"How can that be?" Hurt asked. "The rest of the building is OK."

"I don't know sir," Thomas replied.

"Sorry, I know that. We must be missing something. Obviously whoever created this complex realized that we are not a threat to them and turned on the life support for us. So why not in there?" Hurt stated and then thought a moment. "Lt. Smith respond please."

"Yes Captain," he replied. "I'm here. What is it?" "Listen to me carefully and do exactly as I say," Hurt said. "I need you and your team to put your weapons down somewhere away from the door."

"But sir…" Lt. Smith started.

"Do it," Hurt said. "That's an order."

Lt. Smith and his team placed their weapons in a cabinet at the opposite side of the room from the door.

"Sir," Lt. Commander Thomas said. "Scans indicate life support coming up inside the room. Temperature, atmosphere are all normal now sir."

"Lt. Smith," Hurt stated. "Can you hear me?" "Yes sir," he replied.

"Remove your helmets and step towards the door please," Hurt ordered.

"Aye sir," Lt. Smith replied as he and his team removed them. They walked towards the door and it finally opened.

"Are you all OK?" Hurt said as they entered the corridor.

"Yes sir Captain," Lt. Smith replied. "We're a bit shaken up but other then that we're fine. Do you know what's going on sir?"

"Not entirely," the Captain replied. "But I think we are finally being accepted as non threatening. Hopefully now we'll be able to get some answers. Let's look for some sort of computer interface. Lt. Commander Thomas use your scanner and see if you can locate the source of the power that's controlling the force shield and providing life support."

"Aye Captain," Thomas replied as he manipulated the controls of his scanning unit. "Sir. There's something interfering with the scanners ability to lock onto the exact source. The closest I can say is somewhere under this building."

"Fair enough," Hurt said. "It was to much to hope that they would make it easy for us. We go down then."

The Captain and his team worked their way down deep inside the complex. They checked every chamber and room they came to.

"Anything on the scanner yet?" Hurt asked.

"Still down," Lt. Commander Thomas replied. "Two maybe three levels. I'm sorry, I just can't be sure sir."

"That's fine, it'll just have to do," Hurt stated. "We'll have to keep looking."

They searched the next level without success. As they headed down to the next level Lt. Thomas reported that the scanner failed.

"Understood," Hurt said as they continued on.

The team searched every room, still nothing that resembled a power source. When they reached the final sub-level they found it to be a circular corridor. They split into two teams and searched the rooms, which were all located on the perimeter side of the corridor and then they found, a small door on the interior side of the corridor.

"This must be it," Lt. Commander Thomas said as he started towards the door.

"Hold up a minute," Hurt said and then he activated his communicator. "Hurt to Patton. Do you still have us on sensors?"

"Aye sir," Lt. Tibor replied. "Is there a problem down there sir?"

"Not at this time," Hurt replied. "Our hand scanners quit functioning and I was concerned if you still had us. That's all."

"Understood Captain," Lt. Tibor stated. "Commander Fellows reported that both of the alien shuttles had activated but only one opened up. His preliminary search is still inconclusive at this time sir."

"Understood," Hurt said. "Keep me informed. Hurt out!"

"Aye sir. Patton out," Lt. Tibor said.

"Well Mr. Thomas," Hurt said. "Shall we see what lies behind that door?"

"Yes sir," Lt. Commander Thomas replied.

Lt. Commander Thomas slowly walked up to the door but nothing happened. He stepped back and searched the jams for any switches or controls but found none. Captain Hurt stepped up to the door as well and still nothing happened.

"Hm. I wonder…" Hurt mused. "Everyone put your helmets back on and lower the visors."

After the men had their helmets in place Captain Hurt stepped in front of the door again and it opened up into an airlock. The men entered and the door sealed behind them and after a few seconds the inner door opened. Hurt cautiously entered the chamber followed by his men. It was circular and approximately twenty meters across and six meters high and in the center of the chamber, suspended up off the floor, was a glowing sphere approximately three meters in diameter.

Lt. Commander Thomas instinctively pulled his scanner from his belt and turned it on "Sir!" he exclaimed. "The scanner is working again. I'm reading a total vacuum inside the chamber, radiation within nominal limits. Still unable to determine what the power source is though."

"Thank you Commander," Hurt said and then he activated his communicator. "Hurt to Patton. Do you read me?"

Silence.

Lt. Commander Thomas activated his communicator and said, "Lt. Commander Thomas to Patton. Do read me? Come in Patton."

Still nothing.

"This chamber must be shielded," Thomas stated. "Captain. You better have a look at this," Lt. Smith said as he scanned the room. "I think I may have found the control panel."

The captain and the rest of the team walked over to Lt. Smith's position. He was standing in front of a small console protruding from the wall. Captain Hurt examined the console and saw that there was a representation of the solar system on one section. There was a representation of the planet and the structure that they were in on another section, with lights that corresponded to the ship in orbit and themselves on the planet. And on another section there was a corresponding representation of the other away teams on the other planets. Lt. Commander Thomas reached out his hand and touched the lights that represented the chamber that they were in and a screen came to life on the wall in front of them. On the screen they saw themselves standing in front of the screen.

Captain hurt then reached up and touched the light that represented Commander Fellows away team and instantly he was watching them as they investigated the shuttles that they had found.

"Captain Hurt to Commander Fellows. Do you read me?" Hurt said after activating his communicator.

"I read you loud and clear," Fellows replied. "Are you back on board the Patton?"

"Negative," Hurt said. "We're still on the planet. We've located a power source and a control panel of sorts. We are able to see what you are doing from here though. Proceed with caution."

"Understood," Fellows said. "I was just about to enter the shuttle to see if I could access the computer…"

"Negative Commander!" Hurt stated. "If it's anything like the complex that we're in then it could have an automated launch program and you and your away team could be carried away. Continue recording your scans and rendezvous with the Patton in twenty-four hours. The Duncan will be here in two days. They are better equipped to investigate. Hurt out."

"Acknowledged," Fellows said. "Fellows out."

Commander Fellows scanned the two shuttles for another fifteen minutes before they continued on their way. The size of the underground bay was almost large enough to park the Patton in. The away team was heading for the door and when they were about one hundred meters from it one of the shuttles lifted off as the roof of the hanger bay opened and then the shuttle flew out.

"What the?" Commander Fellows exclaimed. "Commander Fellows to captain Hurt. Do you copy?"

"Hurt here," the Captain responded. "Go ahead Commander."

"Sir, one of the shuttles just took off," Fellows reported.

"Sorry about that," Hurt stated. "That was our fault."

"What? I mean, how's that sir?" Fellows said.

"It appears this control panel has the ability to remotely activate the shuttles," Hurt explained. "Lt. Smith here touched the indicator for one of the shuttles and then we watched as it moved out. I believe it's on its way to us."

"Understood Captain," Fellows remarked. "Try and give us a little warning next time. Fellows out."

"Hopefully there won't be a next time," Hurt said as he glanced at Lt. Smith.

When Commander Fellows and his team were within a few meters of the large door it opened into a large corridor. As they entered the corridor the overhead lights came on ahead of them and they noticed that they turned off behind them when they were a few meters along. The team continued exploring the massive underground facility, recording everything as they went along. When they got to the end of the corridor another large door opened into another large room.

The team entered and the lights came on. Commander Fellows and his team found themselves standing in the main control room of the complex. Screens came to life on the walls and they could see the shuttle that had just launched flying out into space. Another screen showed the Patton as it orbited the ice planet.

"Commander Fellows to Captain Hurt. Come in please," Fellows called out on his communicator.

"Hurt here," came the reply. "What is it Commander?"

"Sir. We have located a control room and we are able to monitor everything," Fellows explained. "Explain "everything"," Hurt said.

"It would appear that this control room is linked up with sensors positioned throughout the solar system," Fellows said. "The screens show all of the planets. We can see the Patton in orbit above you and the shuttle as it heads your way. We have eyes on Lt. Callum's away team as well as you and yours."

"Understood," Hurt said. "Be careful of what you touch and record everything and keep me informed. Hurt out."

"Aye sir," Fellows said. "Fellows out."

Captain Hurt and his team were studying the power room when they saw a flashing yellow light appear on the screen above the small control panel they had found.

"It looks like a ship coming in," Lt. Smith reported. "Is it the Duncan?" Lt. Commander Thomas asked.

"Negative," Smith replied. "It's coming from inside the system. It has to be the shuttle craft."

"Keep an eye on it," Hurt said. "I want to know when and where it lands."

"Aye sir," Lt. Smith replied as he monitored the screen.

One of the crew members approached Lt. Smith, tapped him on the arm and pointed to his suit control. Lieutenant Smith studied the control for a minute.

"Captain," Lt. Smith called out. "We're running low on life support."

The Captain and the rest of the team looked at their suit controls also.

"Everybody out of here," Hurt ordered. "We'll re-fill our suits in the corridor."

The away team entered the airlock and then exited out into the corridor. They opened their visors and re-filled their air tanks. While they waited for the tanks to fill some of the crew took a few minutes to grab a quick snack from their food rations. When everybody's suits were filled they went back into the power room.

A few minutes later Lt. Smith reported that the shuttle was entering the planets almost non-existent atmosphere. "I wish there were a way we could get a visual on that shuttle," Lt. Commander Thomas said.

Lt. Smith reached up and touched the light that was representing the shuttle and suddenly it appeared on the screen while a light appeared on a smaller screen just off to one side. Smith touched the light and its image appeared on the smaller screen as well.

"Captain. We have the shuttle on visual here and over here," Thomas stated as he passed a glance in Lt. Smiths' direction.

"Good work Lt.," Hurt said as he stepped in front of the screen.

They watched as the shuttle broke through the upper cloud layer and headed towards their position on the ice planet. The shuttle was buffeted by the high winds and finally settled down on a large landing platform that appeared to be on top of the building next to the one that they were in. The smaller screen flickered and went blank. Alien writing appeared on the screen and started to slowly scroll down and one of the buttons on the control panel lit up and then started blinking.

"This must be some sort of automated message," Lt. Commander Thomas offered. "This panel must be linked to the landing pad. This button might activate the audio."

"Should I press it?" Lt. Smith asked.

"We don't know for sure," Lt. Commander Thomas stated.

"We might as well see," Hurt said. "Press it and if it is audio; record everything and we'll send it back to Space Fleet for analysis."

"Aye sir," Lt. Smith replied as he pressed the button. An alien voice filled their headsets inside their helmets.

The alien writing on the screen scrolled along as the audio played on. The message lasted about five minutes and then started replaying. The Captain reached over and pressed the button on the panel again and the audio stopped but the writing continued to scroll along.

"Send this to the Vergon home-world," Hurt ordered. "They were the ones who translated the original message. Maybe they can translate this too."

Just then the Captain had an incoming message. "Commander Fellows to captain Hurt," he heard in his headset. "Do you copy?"

"Hurt here," he replied. "Go ahead."

"We're receiving some sort of alien message on one of our screens," Fellows said.

"That would be from the shuttle," Hurt said. "We're seeing it too. It activated the minute the shuttle landed here."

"Understood Captain," Fellows out."

As Lt. Smith studied the screen that the alien writing was on, he noticed a series of five vertical circular designs off to the left of the text. He touched the top circle and the message stopped scrolling. He touched the next circle and the message scrolled back to the top and stopped. He touched the third circle and the message started scrolling again. He touched the fourth circle and the message scrolled to the bottom and stopped and when he touched the last circle the message disappeared and the visual of the shuttle reappeared on the screen.

Lt. Smith touched the bottom circle once again and the screen went blank and then the light reappeared. He touched the light again and the ship reappeared on the screen. When he touched the second circle again the message reappeared.

"I think I'm getting the hang of this," Lt. Smith stated. "Explain," Lt. Commander Thomas said.

"It's a touch-screen. I believe these circular designs control how the screen functions," Smith said. "I noticed them while the message was playing. The top circle pauses the text. The second circle rewinds it. The third circle starts it while the fourth circle fast-forwards it. The bottom circle shuts it off and reverts back to video and when pressed again it just shows the object as a light and so on."

"Did you try any other screen?" Thomas asked. "No sir," Lt. Smith replied. "Just this one."

Lt. Commander Thomas stepped in front of the main screen again and reached out and touched the light indicating Commander Fellows's away team. They appeared on the main screen.

"I don't see any circular designs," he stated.

"This must be the main view screen," Hurt said. "That smaller screen must be for communicating with the shuttles."

"I wonder..." Lt. Smith said. "Captain if I may. I'd like to try something."

"Go ahead Lt.," Hurt said. "Thank you sir," Smith said.

Lt. Smith touched the light on the main screen that represented the Patton in orbit. The light appeared on the smaller screen. Lt. Smith touched the light and the image of the ship appeared.

"We're being hailed sir," Ensign Todd said to Lt. Tibor.

"On screen ensign," Lt. Tibor ordered. "This is Lt. Melissa Tibor of the USS Patton. Come in."

The image of the Patton was replaced by Lt. Tibor's face on the smaller screen.

"Lt. Smith here," Smith said. "We believe we have found the communications control."

"Understood," Lt. Tibor replied. "Do you require anything?"

"Hurt here," the Captain said as he stepped in front of the screen. "We're fine for now Lieutenant. We're trying to understand this technology. Contact us as soon as you hear from the Duncan. They should be here in thirty-six hours. Hurt out."

"Aye sir," Tibor replied. "Patton out."

"Well Lieutenant," Hurt said. "Your hunch paid off about this panel. Now lets see if we can find out how to access the main computer and see if we can find out what happened to the residents of this system."

"Aye sir," Smith said.

The away team found the computer but all that was there were the supervisor's logs from the facility. After nearly an hour of study, it became clear that the structure they were in was used as an observational outpost.

"Our work here is about done," Hurt said. "We might as well get back to the Patton. We'll send everything we've collected back to the Vergons for analysis. When the Duncan gets here they can continue on with the mission."

The Captain and his men made their way up and out of the structure and then beamed back up to the Patton. They headed for the fifth planet and took up a position above the metropolis. The Captain beamed down to where Commander Fellows and his away team were doing their search.

"Captain. Were you able to find out anything?" Fellows asked.

"Not much," Hurt replied. "We believe the planet to be some sort of outpost. Perhaps used to monitor ship traffic through the solar system. We found what appeared to be logs and reports. We're sending them on to Space Fleet for confirmation. What have you found out here so far?"

"We think this was a major space port," Commander Fellows replied. "That landing port out there is big enough to park the Patton on and those screens are linked to sensor arrays throughout the solar system. If it's out there you can probably see it here. Lt. Jones thinks he may have located the main computer control panel too. I was about to contact you when you beamed down."

"Show me what you have found Lt.," Captain hurt said as he walked over to where Lt. Jones was standing.

"Captain. I believe this to be the central control panel for the entire operation of this space port," he explained.

"Have you tried anything yet?" Captain Hurt asked. "No sir. I didn't want to do anything that could put the away teams in danger," he replied.

"A wise decision," Captain Hurt stated as he took out his communicator. "Captain Hurt to the Patton. Have Lt. Callum and his team report back to the ship and standby."

"Aye sir," Lt. Tibor replied. "This just came in.

Captain Pierce has sent us the program from the Vergonians to decipher the alien language. I'm sending it to you now." Lt. Tibor replied.

"Thank you Lt. Tibor," Hurt replied. "Hurt out."

They saw Lt. Callum and his away team lift off as they watched the screens in front of them. Once he was back on board the Patton Captain Hurt stood in front of the control panel.

"I have the program now Captain," Commander Fellows reported.

Captain Hurt took the computer pad and studied it and then he searched the control panel and pressed down on the controls. More screens flickered and came on-line as the main computer booted up. The Captain manipulated more controls and located what appeared to be the diagnostic program.

"Okay. It appears the majority of the inhabitants of this system evacuated some twenty-five years ago," Hurt stated. "A handful of scientists stayed and shut everything down to conserve power and then sent out the automated message. They set up sensors to detect sentient life forms and then they left the planet a few years later. These sensors detected our presence as soon as we entered the solar system and then activated individual sub-systems the minute we entered the solar system and landed on the planets. It's up to us to find out where they went."

"Why did they leave?" Commander Fellows asked. "A spike in the solar radiation coming from the binaries forced them to start an evacuation," Hurt stated. "We need to get out of here…" Fellows started.

"Not necessary," Hurt stated. "The radiation isn't harmful to us. But it was lethal to the previous residents. We're safe."

"Why the message if they didn't plan on sticking around to wait for an answer?" Fellows asked.

"They didn't know how long it would take before the message was intercepted," Hurt said. "Or if it would even be understood when it was. The scientists stayed as long as they could before finally leaving. They buried the coordinates somewhere deep within the main computer…"

Suddenly alarms started going off and red lights flashed on the screen.

"Patton to Captain Hurt. Come in please," Lt. Callum called on the radio.

"Hurt here. What is it?" Hurt replied.

"Ship's sensors have detected a power surge coming from a few satellites in orbit," Lt. Callum explained when the Captain answered.

"We see it on our screens down here too," Hurt said. "I must have activated the planetary defenses when I brought the main computer back on-line."

Commander Fellows noticed a red indicator light coming in from the outer edge of the solar system. When he touched the screen the image of the Duncan appeared. Captain Hurt found the controls and activated the communications panel.

"This is Captain Hurt calling the Duncan. Come in Captain Pierce," he stated.

"Captain Pierce here," came the reply. "What is it Captain Hurt?"

"Do you have your weapons on-line?" Hurt asked. "Yes we do," Pierce replied. "Why?"

"Please take them off-line," Hurt replied. "What's going on?" Pierce asked.

"Trust me Captain Pierce," Hurt replied. "I'll explain everything when you get here. But you must deactivate all your weapons."

"As you wish," Pierce replied. "Done."

Just as suddenly as the alarms started they stopped and the red indicator lights turned yellow. Lt. Callum reported that the satellites had powered down as well.

"Thank you Lt. Callum," Hurt said. "We see it down here too."

"This is Captain Pierce to Captain Hurt," Pierce stated over the radio. "What is going on there?"

"The planets defense system was activated," Hurt explained. "As long as you keep your weapons off-line while you travel through the system you'll be fine."

"Can you deactivate the defense system?" Pierce asked.

"We are still figuring out the controls here," Hurt stated. "Until we figure them out it would be wise to keep our weapons down."

"Understood," Pierce said. "We'll be there in a few hours. Maybe our combined efforts can speed up the process."

"Perhaps it can," Hurt said. "We await your arrival." "Keep me informed if you find something," Pierce said. "Pierce out."

"Understood," Hurt said. "Hurt out."

Captain Hurt and his team continued to study the control panels until the Duncan was in orbit. He called Captain Pierce and then he beamed up to the Duncan and sat down with him and briefed him on all that he and his team had uncovered.

"Welcome to the Duncan Ron," Pierce said as he entered the conference room. "Please sit."

"Thank you Jon," Captain Hurt said as he sat down. "This is quite the ship you have here; a major improvement over the original Duncan A I see. How was the trip?"

"Thank you. It's an amazing ship," Pierce replied. "The trip was fine."

"Any contact with our mystery ship?" Hurt asked. "No. Nothing," Pierce replied. "Whoever they were,

they must not be interested in making contact yet. So Ron. What have you got for me?"

"Right," Hurt started. "Well Jon. As you know from my reports, we detected the automated message when we hit the outer edge of the binary system. The signal jumped from the outer planet to the fifth and then fourth planet when we tried to land at each site. We decided to send teams down to each planet simultaneously and search and that's when the signal ceased transmitting. We discovered the outpost on the outer planet and determined that it must have been used to monitor incoming and outgoing ship traffic. The fourth and fifth planets were inhabited up until the increase in radiation from the suns…"

"Yes we detected the radiation when we entered the system also," Pierce stated.

"Okay. We believe that's when the inhabitants made their decision to evacuate," Hurt explained. "A few scientists remained and set up the signal and then stayed as long as they could before they themselves had to flee. We believe the coordinates to where they headed are stored in the computer. The Patton just doesn't have the ability to retrieve them. I'm afraid of instead of a contact mission this has turned into a detective mission."

"This should make for an interesting first mission," Pierce stated. "We are equipped with the latest computers in Space Fleet. The Vergonians oversaw the programming themselves. I'm certain with all the upgrades we should be able to figure this out."

"Would you like us to stick around and assist?" Hurt asked.

"Thank you Ron," Pierce said. "I appreciate the offer, but you and your crew have been out for a long time.

We're fresh out of dock so why don't you let me know if you need anything and then you go and head back in."

"Thank you Jon," Hurt said. "My crew could use the break. I'll have Commander Fellows put together a list of anything that we might need and we'll go from there."

"Good," Pierce said. "Let me show you around before you head out."

"Great. I'd like that," Hurt said.

And with that Captain Pierce gave Captain Hurt a tour of the newest ship in the Space Fleet line. After Captain Hurt returned from touring the Duncan and the supplies had been stored, the Patton left orbit and headed back in, back to home port.

CHAPTER
EIGHTEEN

The crew of the Duncan spent the next two weeks studying and deciphering the alien language. They eventually discovered that the alien race had headed to a planet that was deep out into uncharted territory. When Captain Pierce contacted Space Fleet and informed them of the location he asked if the ship should go out and investigate. He was given orders to report to the border between Zephyr and Andromidan space. It had been reported that there had been an attack on a League cargo vessel traveling through there by an unidentified ship and it was suspected that the Andromidans were involved somehow.

The Duncan left orbit and headed to the rendezvous point. The Duncan dropped out of light speed and joined up with twelve other ships from Zephyr, Algernon and Archimedes. They took up defensive positions some five hundred thousand kilometers inside League space. They didn't have long to wait. Just two days after their arrival six Andromidan warships de-cloaked only a few thousand kilometers inside their own border.

"That's far enough Commanders," Captain Roselyn Joyce of the U.S.S. Brigand stated on the radio.

"I am Ptaar, Commander of the Andromidan warship Pting," he stated. "Why are you stationed here with so many ships?"

"One of our cargo ships was attacked recently as it passed our boarders and we want answers." Joyce stated. "We know nothing about an attack on one of your ships," Ptaar stated. "We are here to investigate an attack on one of our ships. Do not think that you can get away with this attack."

"We have not attacked anyone," Joyce stated. "We want answers."

"So do we," Ptaar stated. "As I have said. We know nothing of an attack. I think that you are making an excuse to invade our space. Let me speak to the man in charge."

"I am the Captain in charge here," Joyce stated. "I have full authority to speak for Space Fleet. You will speak with me. Now what is this about an attack on one of your ships as well?"

"One of our science vessels was attacked only a few weeks ago," Ptaar stated. "And now we find you here. How do you explain this Captain?"

"We are here for the same reason," Joyce stated. "The Ankara was destroyed only a week before…"

"Then it would appear that we have a new enemy to deal with," Ptaar interupted.

"Give us your findings and we will give you ours," Joyce offered.

"You will give us those findings and we will see about giving you ours," Ptaar stated.

"Very well," Captain Joyce said. "If it will satisfy you…"

"It will be a start," Commander Ptaar interrupted. "Send all of the information to the Pting Lieutenant Mann," Captain Joyce said to her science officer.

A few minutes later Commander Ptaar sent the results of his own scans back to the Brigand. Captain Joyce sent them out to the other ships and they spent several hours going over every detail.

"Commander Ptaar. We can't identify the weapons signature," she stated over the radio. "What can you make of it?"

"We don't recognize it either," Ptaar replied. "It is some type of new energy weapon and it would appear that both of our ships were hit by it and destroyed almost instantly."

"Yes. We got that too," Joyce said. "I believe you are correct when you say that there is a new player in town. I can assure you that we will do whatever we can to find out who is behind these attacks."

"As will we," Ptaar added. "If we discover that your Space Fleet is behind this in any way, we will come down hard on the League."

With that Ptaar closed the channel, turned their ships and sped away before Captain Joyce could respond.

Captain Joyce met with the Captains of the other League ships to discuss the matter a little bit more before sending in her report and heading off to continue their missions.

CHAPTER NINETEEN

Several years later, the crew of the USS Duncan was between systems studying a nebula cloud when they picked up a distress call from a Space Fleet vessel. When they arrived at the coordinates they were shocked by what they had found. Ahead of them they saw the USS Pegasus drifting in space. It had been long overdue and was thought to have been lost with all hands. Its engines were out after hitting a cosmic string and life support was slowly fading.

Some of the more severely injured crew members were transported to the Duncan's sickbay and then teams were sent over to assist with repairs. They fixed the life support, sub-light engines and then they repaired the light drive enough to get the ship running at light speed five.

As they headed back to the nearest Star Base Captain Pierce sat down with Captain Oran to talk.

"I want to thank you Captain Pierce for coming to our aid," Captain Oran said. "It's a good thing that you were in the area."

"Yes and you're welcome," Pierce said. "You are certainly a long way out. What brought you so far out here?"

"I have been on a special mission for Ambassador William Mont of Vergon," Captain Oran stated. "We had picked up a distress call a few days ago and when we arrived we found a Berillion female and a badly damaged ship. She told me that her name was Leah and that she was out here searching for her mate. We were following a new sensor trail when we encountered the cosmic string. I appreciate the help but I am not at liberty to discuss my mission in any great detail. That is for Ambassador William Mont only."

"Understood Captain," Pierce said. "We will be glad to escort you in if you like."

"Thank you Captain Pierce," Oran said. "But you have done enough and once we reach the Star Base and finish making repairs we'll be fine."

"Perfect," Pierce said. "My ship and staff are at your disposal should you need anything until we reach the Star Base."

"Thank you Captain Pierce," Oran said. "I appreciate the offer."

During the flight to the Star Base Leah had been talking with Captain Pierce. She asked him if it would be Okay to stay on board the Duncan.

"Wouldn't you rather go home and be with your family?" Pierce asked.

"I've been in contact with my father and he agrees with my decision," Leah replied. "My husband is out here somewhere and I'm going to continue to search. It's strictly up to you if you let me stick around."

"I have no objections," Pierce said. "We have lots of room."

"Thank you Jon. I'll try and stay out of your way," Leah stated; and with that she went to gather her belongings and transferred them to her new quarters on the Duncan.

CHAPTER TWENTY

When the Pegasus reached Pogh Captain Oran beamed down to talk to William and Gheron.

"Welcome home Oran," Gheron said. "We feared you were lost. What did you learn out there?"

"Thank you. I'm glad to be back," Oran said. "Well we were to the point one time of being only a week behind Robert when we lost his trail. We were running a sensor sweep of the area trying to pick up his trail when we picked up Leah's distress call and had to rescue her."

"Yes I know. She contacted me and told me about it," Gheron said. "Thank you for finding her."

"Any time," Oran said. "We finally picked up a faint trail from the Arrgott and were following it when we hit the cosmic string and our ship was disabled. I believe that we might have found him if it hadn't been for that."

"We are just glad that you made it," William said. "Now. According to your report it appears that Robert might just be heading towards the Huron system. Who do we have near there?"

Gheron checked the computer and said, "It looks like we have the Jason, she's about six months away, and the Duncan, and she's about five months away."

"Leah's on the Duncan," Oran said. "She insisted on going with them. I couldn't stop her."

"Yes. I know," Gheron said. "Captain Pierce is a good man and he has a fine crew. She'll be fine. Should I have Space Fleet contact them to be on the look out for the Arrgott?"

"No," William said. "They both have other missions that are more important. We don't need to distract them with this. Captain Oran how soon will the Pegasus be fully repaired?"

"I was told three weeks," Oran replied.

"Not good enough," William said. "I'll authorize the leave. Get yourself and your crew some rest. In ten days you'll take command of the Jolenar. As soon as you have your gear transferred, you'll go out there."

"Understood sir," Oran said and then he left to see to his new ship.

"He is a good man," Gheron said after Oran left. "Yes. Yes he is," William said. "Did you know that he is part human?"

"Huh. No, no I did not," Gheron replied.

"Yes," William said. "His great great grandmother had met up with a human from Earth, right here on Pogh. They met and one thing led to another."

"Hm. I was not aware that the two species were compatible," Gheron said. "Wait a minute! Did you just say on Pogh?"

"Yes," William replied. "Quite a while ago too I might add."

"Wait. Just how long ago?" Gheron asked. "Because humans have not been here for that long. They do not like the atmosphere that much."

"Well, it has been about three hundred years or so now," William replied.

"Hm. How could that be?" Gheron asked. "As I remember, there were not any humans here that long ago."

"I know of one," William stated.

Gheron looked at William and thought long, trying to remember any humans on Pogh back then before saying, "I have been here most all of the time now and I cannot recall hearing about a human ever being here up until about a hundred and fifty years ago after they joined The League."

"It does not surprise me Gheron," William offered. "You never really thought about him as being a human from Earth."

"Wait a minute!" Gheron exclaimed. "You are talking about…"

"Robert," William stated. "Yes I am."

"How long have you known?" Gheron asked.

"I have had my suspicions for few years now," William replied. "But I was not really sure until just a few minutes ago when we were talking with Oran again. I sensed it in him. I believe the females name was Illia."

"Right. Now that you mention it," Gheron said. "Bob did tell me that he had met a Thorian. But he never told me her name. That cagey bugger."

"I would not be too disappointed in Robert though," William said. "He is a good man."

"I know that William," Gheron said. "Thank you though for saying that."

"Any time old friend," William said. "It would seem that Leah was getting close to finding him when her ship was damaged and Captain Oran found her."

"Yes it does," Gheron said.

"When was the last time you spoke to her? I mean before she was rescued that is," William asked.

"About three years ago," Gheron replied. "She told me that she had been contacted by an old friend with a possible lead as to where Bob was. She said that she was going to check it out and that she would let me know if she found out anything."

"Did she say how old that information was?" William asked.

"Yes. She said it was pretty current," Gheron replied. "She said that she was only about a week maybe ten days behind him. She had sent out an open call stating where she was going and was flying as fast as her ship would go when she ran into trouble."

"That was a close call! Captain Oran must have heard Leah's call and was following the same lead," William said. "It was a lucky thing that the Pegasus was close by."

"Yes indeed," Gheron said. "Only somehow I do not believe it was just luck."

"Yes. Well, ahem, we have a couple of good ships close and now with the Jolenar heading back out there in ten days, we should get results soon," William said.

"I hope so," Gheron sighed. "I hope so."

"Do not worry old friend," William said. "I am sure that we will see Bob soon enough."

"Thank you William," Gheron said. "Now. If you will excuse me, I have work to do."

"Of course," William said as Gheron headed for the door. "I will see you later for dinner tonight."

"Dinner. Right see you then," Gheron said as he left.

CHAPTER
TWENTY ONE

Several months later Gheron was at home sleeping when he received a call; he checked the time, it was three thirty am. 'Now what,' he thought.

"Hello," he said into the com. panel. "This had better be important!"

"It just might be," the voice said. It was William.

Gheron turned on the video feed and said, "Sorry about that. What is it William?"

"We found Robert," William said. "Well. More like Robert found us."

"When? Where?" Gheron asked frantically.

"About a couple of weeks ago," William replied. "He found the Duncan and Leah. It seems that Captain Pierce contacted the League for information on Robert's property a few days ago at his request. And when they ran a search they found an old arrest warrant."

"What? Gheron asked. "Arrest. What is going on?"

"I do not know yet," William replied. "You had better get down here."

"I will be there in twenty minutes," Gheron stated. "See you then."

"Good," William said. "William out."

Gheron was up and out in a flash. When he got to the council building he headed straight for Williams office.

"What have you got William?" Gheron asked.

"It would seem that the old United States government on Earth found out about Bob's covert actions," William started. "They found out that he rescued you and that he had been flying between Earth and Pogh for several years. It appears that was against the law back then so a warrant was issued for his arrest for treasonous actions. It has been sitting in their records ever since. When Captain Pierce contacted the League about Bob they found the old warrant. Captain Pierce has been ordered to bring him back to Earth for a trial."

"That is ridiculous," Gheron said. "It is not against the law to make contact with alien races."

"Apparently it was back in the mid twentieth century on Earth," William said. "Apparently the warrant fell through a few cracks and was never rescinded. Do not worry I am working on a plan to help him."

"Contact President Shelly. Have her tear it up," Gheron stated.

"It's too late for that. Some hack Xenophobic lawyer initiated a suit. It has to go before the Justices," Bill explained.

"Where is he now?" Gheron asked.

"He is coming in from Star Base one-five-one," William replied. "Leah's bringing him in on the Arrgott with Captain Pierce. They should be on Earth in a week or so."

"What are we waiting for?" Gheron asked. "Lets go."

Just then the door chimes sounded and William opened the door. Ktaal was standing there.

"Hello Ambassadors," Ktaal said. "Is it true that you have located Bob?"

"Yes," William replied. "We are on our way to Earth." "Not without me," Ktaal said. "He is my friend as well.

We will go together."

"OK. Lets go," Gheron said this time. "We will prepare on the way."

"Prepare for what?" Ktaal asked.

"Apparently Bob has been arrested for violating an old Earth law," William replied. "We should get there shortly after he does."

With that, they were on their way to Earth.

The trial was nearly over when the three of them entered the courtroom. They each one gave their testimony and when they were finished it only took a matter of minutes before the justices dropped all charges against Bob and he was set free.

Several weeks later when Bob and Leah arrived at Bob's farm, there was a celebration, Bob's friends and family were there and it was a happy reunion.

William stayed for a few days after everyone had gone on their way, he brought Bob up to speed on what had transpired over the past three hundred and so years since his departure from Earth.

Bob was surprised and somewhat reluctant to accept that he had any part of the League's growth. Bill was sure to let him know just how important a role he had played in its start and growth. Still, Bob was humble and finally accepted the fact that maybe, just maybe, he did have some hand in the League's formation…

www.ingramcontent.com/pod-product-compliance
Lightning Source LLC
LaVergne TN
LVHW011711060526
838200LV00051B/2855